THE TOMBOYS OF CHERRY LANE

THE TOMBOYS OF CHERRY LANE

By Morgan Flynn

The Press at Cal Poly Humboldt

Editing, typesetting, and layout by Wilder Yaconelli
Cover design by Sarah Godlin

ISBN: 978-1-962081-19-1

The Press at Cal Poly Humboldt
California State Polytechnic University, Humboldt
University Library
1 Harpst Street
Arcata, California 95521-8299
press@humboldt.edu
press.humboldt.edu

This is a work of fiction. Any similarities between any persons, living or
dead, is purely coincidental.

Dedicated to the Seattle Women's Field Hockey Team, 2020-2021, who made three years, five days and two surgeries worth it.

CHAPTER 1

Welcome to the Neighborhood

*I*sn't it funny how five years can seem like an eternity? To a child, five years seems an unbridgeable gap. To a teen, five years is the difference between the beginning of your teens and the beginning of legal adulthood. By the time you hit your twenties, five years, the once unbridgeable gap, has lost its power.

My name is Morgan and this is my story. I was seven when we moved into the house on Cherry Lane in Santa Clara, California. We came from Sacramento, but don't ask me about Sacramento because I don't remember much. I do remember the house on Cherry Lane in a neighborhood within a few miles of a naval air station where everybody's father worked. Before the houses were built there had been orchards. Almost every street was named after a fruit, nut, or flower. We were renting the house on Cherry Lane while my parent's dream home was being constructed some five miles away. The new house was a four-bedroom two story, the first up from the corner on a slope. I was getting a room of my own. For now, I shared a room with my sister Laura. We would also have a playroom and best of all, there would be a swimming pool in the backyard. My mother liked the dream house because it had a big kitchen and a formal dining room. She liked to cook and entertain. Dad liked the new house because it made Mom happy.

But I'm getting ahead of myself. The new house was nothing more than a dirt lot when we moved into the rental house. It was March, a week after my seventh birthday and three days before my sister's tenth birthday. The rental house smelled of fresh paint and was filled with cardboard boxes.

Mom told us to unpack only what we needed, because we would only be there a year at most. It was a Saturday. Dad had taken Laura shopping for a new bicycle — it was a birthday present for her — and I was organizing my Hot Wheels collection when the doorbell rang. A few minutes later, Mom called me to come meet the neighbors.

The neighbors were a middle-aged woman with dark hair cut in a bob and her daughter who had dark hair pulled back in a ponytail. The daughter was about a foot taller than me and had freckles like I did.

"This is my daughter Morgan," Mom gestured to me. "Morgan, this is Mrs. Mathews, who lives across the street, and her daughter Suzy. Suzy is twelve going on thirteen and will be babysitting you and Laura sometimes." Mom then explained that Dad had met Mrs. Mathews a week earlier when they came to the neighborhood to sign the rental lease on the house. Mrs. Mathews saw the moving van the day before and knew we had arrived.

"Hi," I said.

"Hi," said Suzy. She grinned at me. "I like your sweatshirt!"

I looked down at myself. I was wearing jeans and the Wonder Woman sweatshirt I got for my birthday.

"Thanks!" I said, noticing that Suzy was also dressed in jeans and a sweatshirt except hers was plain gray. I continued my inspection of her attire. "I like your shoes," I said. She was wearing black Converse high-tops.

"Thanks!" Suzy grinned. "They're boys!"

Mom and Mrs. Mathews exchanged a smile. Mrs. Mathews told Mom how Suzy, a consummate tomboy, went through girl's sneakers and clothes at an alarming rate, so Mrs. Mathews bit the bullet and let her wear boy's sneakers, jeans, and sweatshirts for play clothes that were hand-me-downs from her older brother Rick.

Mom looked at me. "I should think about that for Morgan. She goes through shoes quickly too."

"Cool!" Suzy beamed. "It'll be cool to have another girl wearing boy's sneakers in the neighborhood!"

Mom gave us popsicles and sent us into the front yard to get to know each other. As we sat on the lawn under the shade of a walnut tree Suzy told me about herself and her family. She was the middle child and the only girl. Rick was eighteen and had just joined the Navy. Her younger brother Butch was nine about to turn ten making him the same age as my sister. According to Suzy, Butch was a pain in the butt. Suzy said every kid in her family had dark hair and dark eyes. You couldn't tell one from another in the baby pictures they had up on the walls of their house unless

Suzy was in a dress, which wasn't very often. Later, I learned that Suzy's mother said she'd be happy to give us Suzy's outgrown girl clothes. That made me happy, because my sister Laura was a total girlie-girl who wore a lot of pink, flowers, and unicorns. I hated pink — something told me Suzy wasn't one of the "pink" girls.

Around the time Laura had turned nine, all she wanted to talk about were horses and boys. I didn't care for either. I said as much to Suzy, who agreed with me that horses were not the be-all-end-all that so many other girls thought they were. She told me boys, when they were your older brother, weren't so bad.

Suzy said Rick had taught her to play every sport he knew. If it involved a ball that could be thrown, kicked, or hit, Suzy could do it. She also knew how to tackle and block in football, how to shoot marbles, catch frogs, do tricks with a yo-yo, swim, and how to ride a bike. I didn't know how to do most of those things. Suzy offered to teach me. Laura never wanted to do anything but play Barbies and I didn't like that at all. We were sisters with nothing in common, we didn't even look alike. Laura had brown eyes and black hair like our mother, and I had sandy brown hair and green eyes like Dad – the freckles were a mystery. I was the only one in the family that had them.

We had been in the neighborhood for about a week when Dad took Laura to the bike store to pick up her new bike, a pink three-speed that had to be specially ordered for her. I was getting Laura's old bike, a bottle green 20-inch Schwinn. I rode a red 16-inch wheeler with training wheels that had belonged to Laura once. As I was seven now my parents decided I was too old to have training wheels. My parents drove this home when they gave my bike away then tried to teach me how to ride the 20-inch bike. They weren't very patient. It scared me when I couldn't balance and I cried a lot — which made them angry.

"I don't know what's wrong with you!" Mom yelled at me when I fell over for the umpteenth time. We were on the driveway, having just attempted to ride down the street. It was a Saturday afternoon and it seemed like the whole neighborhood was out washing cars and mowing lawns so I had quite an audience.

"You should be able to do this!" Dad scowled.

"I don't want to do this," I bawled, recoiling from the bike that was causing me so much grief. It was lying on its side in the driveway. "I don't want to do this anymore!" I screamed and I ran into the house.

I was in my room crying when my mother came in and told me to go outside and pick up my bike.

"Your father and I are not going to pick up after a quitter," she snarled, her voice dripping with disdain. "Your father and I have discussed it. No television for you until you learn to ride that bike."

No television was the worst punishment that could be handed down to a seven-year-old.

"No Saturday morning cartoons?" I gasped.

"No! Not until you learn to ride that bike! Now go out there and get it off the driveway and put it back in the garage where it belongs!" Mom shouted.

Tail between my legs, I went back out to the driveway. The bike was still laying there, mocking me. Out of frustration I kicked the back wheel twice.

"Why are you beating up your bike?" Suzy was suddenly

standing behind me. I about jumped out of my skin. I had been so focused on what I was doing I hadn't heard her approach. I turned around to face her, my eyes welling with tears.

"Oh!" Suzy exclaimed. She dropped to one knee in front of me and placed her hands on my shoulders. "Don't cry, it's okay! I'm not going to tell! Why are you beating up the bike?"

"I don't want to ride that bike," I blubbered. "My parents are mad at me because I can't ride a bike."

"Shhh... I don't think they're mad at you?" Suzy gently corrected me, using the cuff of her sweatshirt sleeve to wipe away my tears.

"Yes, they are. I'm a quitter and they don't like quitters, especially Mom!" I sobbed.

Suzy's face hardened. "I don't think she meant that. You'll learn in your own time."

"No television until I learn to ride a two-wheeler," I replied, starting to cry harder.

Suzy blinked. "That's harsh," she said, pulling me in for a hug.

I cried for a few more minutes, then Suzy told me to put the bike in the garage and to come right back. I parked the bike next to Dad's workbench and when I came back outside Suzy was standing there with a smile on her face and her hand on the handlebars of a black 16-inch BMX style bike. She had run across the street to get it. She explained that it had belonged to Butch before he graduated to the 20-inch Stingray that had belonged to Suzy, and before her, Rick.

"The problem is that a 20-inch bike is too much to learn on." Suzy said patiently. "After you learn to ride the 16-incher you can transition to the 20-incher."

"Are you sure?" I started to tear up again.

"It's how I learned," she said, her eyes darting around nervously. "Come with me, we're going to need privacy for this." She grinned at me, and her eyes danced as she said, "Let's surprise your parents."

We walked to the elementary school that was six blocks away. Suzy grinned as she explained that Rick taught her to ride a two-wheeler on the soccer field.

"Grass is much softer than cement, so if you fall over, you don't get hurt," she said.

Getting to the school meant crossing a busy street, something I had been forbidden to do unless the school crossing guard was there. I mentioned this to Suzy, who nodded then led me all the way to the traffic light two blocks away from the crosswalk. Suzy demonstrated how to use the traffic signal button and the crosswalk, telling me that I needed to walk my bike when I used it. I was in awe of such wisdom.

I spent the rest of the day learning to ride the two-wheeler. Suzy ran next to me helping me by holding the handlebars and the back of the seat. Several times she let go, and if I lost my balance she quickly grabbed hold again. I fell over a few times. The first time I went down I recoiled, afraid she would yell at me like Dad had, but Suzy just laughed and threw herself to the ground next to me shouting, "We're tomboys! Falling down is fun!"

"What's a tomboy?" I asked.

"It's a girl that likes to do fun stuff like climb trees and play sports." Suzy explained as she stretched out on the grass. She was a little out of breath because she had been running a lot. She gestured to her jeans and sneakers. "Tomboys wear jeans and get to wear boy's sneakers and play in the creek! We shoot marbles and build forts and even catch frogs and tadpoles!"

That all sounded like fun to me. I looked at her. "Does that mean we don't have to play with dolls?"

Suzy made a disgusted face. "Not if we don't want to."

"Good," I nodded. "I want to be a tomboy then."

Suzy grinned and patted me on the shoulder. "You'll make a good one. I'll teach you." She got to her feet as she said, "Starting with riding a two-wheeler." She picked the bike up and gestured for me to climb on again.

Pretty soon Suzy was just holding on to the seat sometimes, then she let go and ran next to me shouting encouragement. I was getting a few minutes of solo riding — and I fell down a few more times, but I got right back up. Suzy cheered that too.

By the end of the afternoon I was riding all by myself, and Suzy was running next to me hooting and hollering and jumping up and down. She almost seemed more excited than I was. Suzy insisted I ride the bike home — she jogged next to me. As we came around the corner Suzy's parents were standing on our driveway with my parents— both sets of parents were wondering where their daughters were. As I came pedaling up the adults started to applaud.

"Morgan! You're riding a two-wheeler!" Mom exclaimed like I didn't know I was doing it. I braked and got off the bike.

"Suzy taught me!" I said proudly.

Suzy, out of breath because she'd been running, leaned over with her hands on her knees and grinned.

Dad and Mom looked at Suzy. Mr. Mathews nodded his approval and Mrs. Mathews was positively beaming with pride. Mr. Mathews put his hand on Suzy's back and said proudly "That's my girl!"

CHAPTER 2

Tomboy in Training

I became Suzy's shadow, because I could keep up with her now. Suzy rode her bike everywhere, and she rode fast. I learned to ride fast too. Suzy showed me the creek and the best places to catch tadpoles and frogs, the best trees for climbing (also by the creek), how to throw a football (always position your fingers over the laces), how to shoot marbles (knuckles down, no hunching), and most importantly that spring, she taught me how to play baseball. Suzy organized baseball games at the bus stop before school. I learned how to hit, field, and run. The boys always brought their gloves— and one brought a bat. Suzy let me borrow her old glove and she used Rick's old glove. The other girls— who Suzy called the "horse phase girls" including my sister— didn't join in. Laura didn't like me playing baseball because it was such a boy thing to do. She said my behavior shamed the family, so much so it would have been better had I not been born. I didn't like Laura at all, so the words didn't really hurt, but Suzy took great offense when Laura said it in front of her.

We didn't play together at school because Suzy was in the sixth grade, and their classrooms and playground were on the opposite side of the school from the primary grades. Suzy was also one of the sixth graders who had a job chaperoning the lower grades before school and at recess and lunch. They were called Playground Patrol officers. On the day they had duty they wore a reflective green sash over their clothes that read "PLAYGROUND PATROL". Suzy had the duty on Tuesdays. Suzy told me they had to apply for the job, and their classmates had to vote for them. She was fiercely proud that she had been chosen.

Away from school we spent lots of time together, so much so that we became known as The Tomboys of Cherry Lane. The whole neighborhood called us that. Both of us were proud of it. Suzy's mom thought it was cute. My mom hoped it was a phase I would grow out of. I didn't know what that meant.

I quickly figured out that being a tomboy set me apart from other girls. It started when I had to pick my "special study project" in class. The special project consisted mostly of us reading about the topic and drawing pictures of what we read about in a notebook. The options were "Flowers," "Dinosaurs," and "Hot, Cold and Weather." I chose dinosaurs because I thought that was the most interesting. Mrs. Graf, the teacher, tried to get me to choose flowers, saying all the other girls were studying flowers, and I didn't want to be different from the other girls, did I? I said I'd rather study dinosaurs. Mrs. Graf sort of shook her head. She was a big lady with white hair and black horn-rimmed glasses.

She looked mean even when she was smiling. I found the project boring. Because I already knew how to write, instead of just drawing pictures I made up stories about the dinosaurs. I gave them names and had them go on adventures, and I added the stories to the pictures. Mrs. Graf was not impressed and wrote "Dinosaurs didn't do this" across the top of the pages.

When you are different, people will pick on you, even girls. There were three girls that made my life miserable: Nancy Dane, Kiki Barton and Julie Korn. Nancy was the biggest kid in my class because she had been held back — she was almost eight years old and still in the first grade. She was chubby with short blonde hair and glasses. I hadn't been at school for more than a week when she stole my milk money out of my desk and helped herself to my lunch. I told Mrs. Graf, who replied that Nancy would leave me alone if I was more like the other girls, therefore it was my fault that she was picking on me. It would help if I wore more dresses to school — she even called my mother to tell her that.

Kiki and Julie were the self-appointed most popular girls in the class. Kiki was blonde with blue eyes and glasses and Julie had dark hair and eyes. They reminded me of Barbie dolls that have the same features but different hair and eye color. They always dressed alike and were crazy about horses and bragged about their identical, white Schwinn bicycles with banana seats and colored streamers on the handlebars. We rode the school bus together and they made fun of me for playing baseball.

One April morning all three of them decided to gang up on me as we were standing outside our classroom waiting for Mrs. Graf. Kiki started it by commenting on the new purple high-top

Converse sneakers I was wearing. Mom agreed to allow me to wear sneakers provided I would wear a dress to school one day a week. Today was that day. I was wearing a purple dress that matched the sneakers.

"You're wearing boy's sneakers and a dress. You're a boy in a dress," Kiki snarked.

"No, I'm not."

"You're wearing boy's sneakers." Julie joined in.

"Doesn't mean I'm a boy." I bristled.

"Morgan is a boy in disguise," Nancy hooted. "A boy in a dress."

"I'm not a boy!" my voice rose.

"Do you fight like a boy?" Nancy asked as she pushed me into Kiki and Julie.

Kiki and Julie shoved me back into Nancy, who started slapping me. She grabbed the collar of my dress and held on, yelling "You're gonna pay for running into me!"

I kicked Nancy as hard as I could. And I mean HARD. I nailed her in the shin. She cried out and let go of me and dropped to one knee.

"You're going to pay for that!" she screamed, rubbing her shin.

Before she stood up I made a fist and swung as hard as I could. I caught her in the jaw with a right uppercut. There was a loud CRACK! and Nancy went tumbling backward. My classmates gasped, and Julie and Kiki jumped in and startled windmilling, pummeling me with their fists. I didn't hold back. Julie got punched in the stomach so hard that it knocked the wind out of her. She doubled over, crying.

Kiki shrieked at me, grabbing the sleeve of my dress so hard she ripped it. I punched her in the face, a couple of quick jabs. A lens popped out of her glasses and blood spurted from her nose.

The boys were cheering and applauding wildly as I stood there, shaking with rage, when I heard a familiar voice yell "Break it up!" I turned around to see Suzy standing there, wearing her "Playground Patrol" sash. Her eyes were hard with anger.

"Is it Tuesday?" I asked, surprised to see her.

Suzy's eyes went wide, and she shook her head as if she could not believe what she was seeing. "Come with me," she grabbed me by the arm.

"You're going to the office," she announced, making my classmates do that 'Ohhhhhhhhh!' thing that kids did when someone was in trouble. Going to the office was never a good thing. I'd heard about spankings and suspensions and expulsions, and I knew I didn't want any of them. I burst into tears as Suzy frog-marched me to my doom. On the way there we passed a teacher who gave Suzy a "what the hell is this?" look. Suzy told her there were three more casualties by the first-grade classroom. The teacher rushed off to tend to them.

I was full-on bawling, and Suzy cried out, "Oh crap, Morgan stop crying!"

"I'm scared," I blubbered, wiping my eyes with the backs of my hands. That's when I got a stabbing pain in my right wrist. "Ow!" I cried, jerking to a halt.

"What?" Suzy stopped abruptly and turned to face me. She did a double-take. "Your dress is ripped!"

"I know," I cried, gingerly holding my injured limb. "And my wrist hurts!" It was swelling and turning green and purple, and my knuckles were cut up and bruised.

Suzy's eyes went wider.

"Oh no!" She gasped as she reached for my wrist, gently taking it in her hands. She turned my wrist over slowly cringing in sympathy as I gasped and winced when pain ran up my arm.

"Ow!" I cried, trying to pull away from her. "That hurts!"

"I think you broke your wrist!" Suzy exclaimed. "Or maybe sprained it? Let's get some ice on it."

The next thing I knew I was sitting in the principal's office with a frozen sponge held against my wrist with a towel while I waited for my parents. Kiki, Julie, and Nancy were brought in and placed in the nurse's office. All three of them were walking like they were in pain.

Suzy stayed with me because she could tell I was scared.

"Do you want to tell me what happened?" Mr. Paris, the principal, asked wearily. I explained that they were picking on me because of my sneakers and calling me a boy.

"They picked on her even though she's wearing a dress," Suzy said like it was important. "Three against one." She had witnessed the altercation from a distance and came running over to break it up. "They tore her dress, and she might have a broken arm?" Suzy explained, gesturing to my injured limb. "Look how swollen it is!"

Suzy was sent back to class. A few minutes later, my parents showed up.

Mr. Paris told my parents that I had seriously hurt the other girls. Dad replied, "Good for Morgan!" Dad was in the Marines for eight years and he valued strength and standing up for yourself.

Mom scolded me for fighting and wanted to know the details.

I explained that Nancy had been picking on me for a few weeks, and that Mrs. Graf hadn't done anything about it. Kiki and Julie, I said, were just plain mean.

I was sent home for the rest of the day. Dad stayed at school to talk to the other parents while Mom, shaking her head in disapproval, took me to the doctor where I got my first x-rays. I had a sprained wrist. I got a bandage and a splint to wear for a week. Nancy, Julie, and Kiki were suspended for two days and made to pick up trash on the playground for a week. All three had to write letters of apology to me. Dad told Nancy's parents that if she ever harassed me in any way again not only would he permit me to REALLY fight back, he would sue them for all they were worth. I think he made a similar threat to Julie and Kiki's parents because they left me alone for the rest of the year.

A week after the fight the school made me take a bunch of tests because they could tell I was bored in the first grade. It turned out I had a high IQ and that was part 'of the problem'. As a result, I was promoted to the fourth grade for a few hours each day. While the first grade was doing "See Spot Run" I was reading *Where the Red Fern Grows* and *Island of the Blue Dolphin*. Mom said the other girls had picked on me because they could tell I was smart and they were intimidated, but maybe it would help if I learned to play with dolls. I said I didn't want to do that, and Mom just shook her head.

Suzy never came right out and told me she was proud of me for defending myself, but she did tell me that I had sprained my wrist because I had not used proper form when I threw the punches.

When my wrist healed, she brought me into her garage where they had a heavy bag hanging. She taught me how to throw a punch.

"Don't bend your wrist, keep it straight," she said, demonstrating, then she gave me a look and made me promise not to tell my parents she had taught me how to fight.

CHAPTER 3

The Bad Day

*W*ork continued on the new house. On weekends we had family picnics in the house under construction or in the backyard next to the big pit that was soon to be a swimming pool. Sometimes we went to water the oak trees that were next to the house. They had mattresses around them to protect them during the construction. Dad said the house would be ready by late summer.

One Saturday afternoon when we got home from the new house our next-door neighbor Mrs. Schapper met us on the driveway. She said the Navy Chaplain had been to the Mathews house and she feared for the worst. Dad's face hardened and he sent me and Laura inside with Mrs. Schapper, asking her to watch us for a few minutes so he and Mom could go see the Mathews family.

Mom and Dad came back about a half hour later. Mom was crying as she told us that Rick Mathews had been killed in a training accident. Dad got down on one knee and placed his hands on my shoulders to tell me that Suzy had taken off running when she learned Rick was dead. Her parents and Butch were at home while the rest of the neighborhood was out looking for Suzy – did I have an idea where she could be? It would be dark soon and they were very worried.

I felt very grown-up as I listed the places where I would look for Suzy: her tree house in the backyard, the rope swing hanging from big oak tree next to the creek, the frog pond located on the edge of golf course, the vacant lot behind the Safeway and the soccer field at our school. Mrs. Schapper went to spread the word to the neighbors about where to look and Dad grabbed a flashlight to join the search party. I was scared and worried and I tried to stay awake until Dad got home but I guess I fell asleep, because the next thing I knew there was sunlight streaming through the bedroom window.

Over breakfast Dad told us that the men in the neighborhood had spent most of the evening looking for Suzy. She was found sitting on a log down by the creek around 9:30 at night. She was shivering because she didn't have a jacket. Dad said she was in shock. I didn't know what that meant, but from the way my parents looked, I figured it was bad.

Rick's funeral was held a few days later. Dad went while Mom and Mrs. Schapper went to the Mathews' house and set it up like for a party, except it wasn't a happy occasion. Dad called it a wake, which he said was sort of a reception that you held after a funeral. There were lots of people dressed in black gathering in small groups talking and telling stories about Rick. Mom made a casserole and a batch of oatmeal cookies for the wake. From the amount of food on the Mathews' dining room table, I think every person in the neighborhood made something.

The furniture in the house had been re-arranged, and all the photographs with Rick in them had been taken down. The Mathews family was all dressed in black. Suzy was wearing a dress — and her black sneakers. Mom wanted me to talk to Suzy, saying the Mathews were worried because Suzy wasn't saying much at all. I went looking for her and found her in the backyard sitting on the wooden picnic table next to the walnut tree that held the tree house she had built with Rick when she was six.

"Hi," I said timidly as I walked up.

Suzy tossed a glance over her shoulder. "Hi," she said. Her voice was broken and her face tear stained. "Thanks for coming."

"I'm sorry for your loss," I delivered the line my parents told me to say at the wake. Kids weren't allowed at the funeral.

"Thanks," She wiped her face with her right hand.

"I'm surprised you're not up in your tree house?" I remarked, knowing it was one of Suzy's favorite places.

"I promised my mom I wouldn't climb trees in a dress," Suzy explained.

"Oh."

There was an awkward pause broken when Suzy choked on a sob. "I'm not crying," she wailed.

"Sure you are," I said reproachfully. I placed a hand on her shoulder trying to comfort her.

"No, I'm not!" she snapped, looking at me sharply. She could sure look mean when she wanted to, and I backed up, a little afraid.

"It's okay to cry," I said finally. "We're tomboys, we can do anything we want to!"

Suzy started to cry and laugh at the same time. "We can?"

"Sure," I shrugged. "Anything! That includes crying."

"What idiot told you that?" Suzy demanded.

I thought for a moment. "You did?"

Suzy cried harder, then she sort of chuckled as she said, "Then I guess I should take my own advice, eh?"

That summer, the Mathews family moved to the other side of town. I was away at summer camp and when I came home and found out Suzy was gone it seemed like a betrayal. She didn't mention they were moving, but it's not like I saw much of her after Rick died. The whole family sort of closed ranks. Mom said they couldn't stand being in the house because everything reminded them of Rick. Two weeks later we moved into the new house. In September Laura and I would start classes at a new elementary school, and we would eventually go to the same middle school and high school as the Mathews and the rest of the kids from the neighborhood.

CHAPTER 4

He's Thirteen, He's My Brother

*O*ur new house was nine blocks from the middle school and high school and six blocks from where the Mathews family had moved. Mom and Dad were still friends with Mr. and Mrs. Mathews because they belonged to a social club called the Gourmet Group. Once a month they had a big dinner party focusing on a native dish of a particular country. Us kids were told to be scarce when our parents hosted.

One Memorial Day my parents had a pool party. The Gourmet Group, including the Mathews family were among the guests.

Laura, who was thirteen, couldn't wait to see Butch in his swim trunks. I couldn't wait to see Suzy, who was now in high school. For the party she was wearing gold athletic shorts and a gray Wilson High athletics T-shirt. Her long dark hair was up in a ponytail. As we ate ice cream at the kitchen table, she told us about being on the field hockey and basketball teams and doing the long jump on the track team. She had set a new school record in the long jump and earned her letter for it.

I hung on Suzy's every word, but Laura was distracted by Butch, wearing cutoff jeans as bathing trunks, jumping off the diving board and into the pool. Laura turned to Suzy and asked, "Have you noticed if Butch has any chest hair?"

At that very moment Suzy had a mouth full of vanilla ice cream. Suzy's eyes went wide and she swallowed with some difficulty. She looked at my sister with an expression of pure dismay as she replied, "He's thirteen. He's my brother."

I was not sure what this meant. Apparently, Laura didn't know what it meant either, because she paused momentarily, then proceeded to ask another more intimate question about Butch's anatomy.

Unfortunately, Suzy had another spoonful of ice cream in her mouth. Suzy gagged and dropped her spoon so it clattered on the table. She grabbed a paper napkin to cover her mouth and swallowed. The red started to climb to her face as she repeated, enunciating each word slowly and carefully, "He's thirteen. He's my brother." Suzy's dark eyes hardened, non-verbally communicating her distaste for this line of questioning. This should have been a clue that boundaries were being crossed. Sadly, for my sister, it was not.

Laura proceeded to ask another question; this one was the Queen Mother of inappropriate questions. It was a question that someday, Butch's wife would know the answer to. It was a question that someday, Butch's girlfriend would probably know the answer to. It was a question that Butch's sister should NOT know the answer to, unless there was something grave and seriously wrong with the family dynamic.

I swear Suzy was shaking. She closed her eyes tight, cringing as if she was in physical pain. She was bright red, and her shoulders were hunched around her ears and she was holding her hands on either side of her head as if she was expecting to cover her ears to protect them from an explosion. With her eyes still closed she rasped, "He's thirteen. He's. My. Brooooooooother!" She sounded like a wounded animal caught in a trap.

Laura looked perplexed and tossed me a look. I shrugged. The question was about a body part I had never heard of before, but from Suzy's reaction I determined that it was a body part you shouldn't talk about. Laura, oblivious to the pain she had inflicted, stared at Suzy, waiting for her to answer.

Suzy, still blushing with her eyes closed, was gasping for air like a goldfish suddenly liberated from the bowl.

"Hey Suzy, you wanna come see my fort on the side of the house?" I heard myself ask.

Suzy's eyes flew open and she slammed her palms down on the kitchen table as she leapt to her feet crying out, "GOD YES!"

I went out the back door with Suzy on my heels. The fort was a ten-by-six-foot wooden structure on the side of the house along the fence line. It had a bunk, bookshelves, a periscope, a window, and a hatch so I could climb on to the roof. The fort was everything from my pirate ship to my log cabin on the prairie to my B-25 *The Flyer Nine*. But at that very moment, the fort was a respite for the highly uncomfortable teenager following close behind me.

"This is it," I said as I lifted the latch to open the door. "I built it with my dad."

Suzy didn't respond. She stormed over to the bunk and sat down hard. She was staring into space, as she brought her hands up again on either side of her ears — still waiting for that explosion. She was still shaking her head slightly. Her face was still red. She was struggling to form words. I knew this was BAD.

"I'm going to go up on the roof." I said awkwardly. I went up the ladder through the hatch to the roof. Since our house was on a slope, I had a commanding view of the neighborhood. I had been up there for a few minutes, pondering what had happened in the kitchen when I heard Suzy coming through the hatch. She joined me, sitting so she could swing her long legs off the edge. Her face had returned to a normal color, and she no longer wore the expression of someone who had just witnessed a car accident.

"Are you okay?" I asked, a little frightened.

"Yeah," she sighed, as she put her hand over her eyes and sort of shook her head as she muttered, "That was so inappropriate! I cannot believe your sister was asking those questions!"

"Neither can I," I said. "I think she likes Butch."

"Yeah, that's been established," Suzy said, removing her hand from her eyes and making a dismissive gesture. "But... I cannot believe she was asking those things!" She shook her head slowly, eyes widening in horror and dismay.

There was an awkward silence, then I blurted out, "I don't know what she was talking about."

Suzy looked at me, somewhat surprised. "You don't?"

"No." I replied. "There are only girls in this family. I don't know anything about... that."

Suzy looked uncomfortable. "Do you want me to explain it to you?" she asked, as if she dreaded what my answer would be.

"God no!" I squeaked. I shook my head empathetically as I added, "I'm only ten! Boys are still icky!"

Suzy let out a loud sigh of relief and placed a hand on my shoulder. "Thank God!" she cried, gazing skyward.

CHAPTER 5

Sports Are My Salvation

$\mathcal{I}$ played on school teams in part because Suzy did. Suzy was a three sport girl and I wanted to be one too. In middle school I went out for flag football, soccer and threw the discus on the track team. I was the first girl in my class to earn a letter. My grades were good, and I was happy.

Laura was resentful. She said I played sports as an excuse to watch the girls in the shower after practice. All tomboys did, she said. I knew I didn't do that — did other girls? I asked Suzy about it. Suzy got angry, calling Laura a liar. She must have said something to her mother, because Mrs. Mathews called Mom, saying she didn't appreciate Laura's inappropriate remarks about her children. Mom apologized and scolded Laura, then told me that just to be safe I should try to be more feminine and develop interests besides sports. Dad suggested music lessons, specifically guitar. He was sore because a year earlier Laura had asked for guitar lessons and he bought a guitar for her. She quit after a month. So I had guitar lessons twice a week from five to six in the evening after football, soccer or track practice, depending on the season.

The middle and high school teams practiced at a sports complex located between the schools. It had a football stadium, a track and field venue, two athletic fields used for soccer and field hockey, a baseball and softball diamond and two gymnasiums. Suzy was there with the high school teams and on days I didn't have guitar lessons we walked home together, her in her black and gold letterman jacket and me in my red and white sweat jacket with a red block H for Hoover Middle School. Our friendship was rekindled as we often took the long way home along the creek path. We talked about things we couldn't talk about with anyone else. Suzy told me how she threw herself into sports because it gave her something to focus on after Rick died. I told her how much I hated being at home because of Laura and Mom, and how glad I was that sports and guitar gave me someplace to go.

My sister, it seemed, had nothing to do after school but get into trouble. One day I came home to fire trucks in front of our house. Laura had invited her friends over to raid my parents' liquor cabinet. They got drunk, and when they tried to smoke cigarettes they accidentally set the living room carpet on fire.

My parents were at work when it happened. Laura tried to blame it on me, but I had been at football practice. The carpet and part of the ceiling had to be replaced. Dad said we were lucky we didn't lose the whole house. Mom justified Laura's behavior by saying the ages of twelve to fifteen were "the jungle age" when kids did stupid things.

As if to prove it, a week later fourteen-year-old Butch Mathews stole Suzy's car late Saturday night and went speeding around the neighborhood with his buddies. Butch lost control going around a curve and crashed it in a neighbor's yard. Mr. Mathews called Dad the next morning for help -- the car was stuck in a hedge. Dad had a big truck with a tow chain for situations just like this. I asked to go with him because I thought Suzy would be there, and I thought I could comfort her. When we got there we learned Mrs. Mathews had locked Suzy in her room to keep her from killing her little brother. Dad, looking at the tire tracks leading to the impact, figured Butch was doing over 80 mph when he hit the curb. The car was a brown Ford five-speed station wagon that had been the family transportation until Suzy turned sixteen and got her driver's license and Mrs. Mathews upgraded to a Volvo sedan. The grill of the Ford was bent, and juniper boughs were stuck in it. Both front tires were flat, and at least one of the wheel rims looked bent. It was high centered on a stump half buried in the hedge. The police were there talking to the homeowner. He'd heard the crash and got a good look at the fleeing boys. It was easy to track down the owner of the car and now Butch was sitting in the back of the police cruiser looking angry with scratches and bruises on his face.

Dad attached one end of the chain to the station wagon and the other to the truck and pulled it off the stump. Two other neighbors helped Mr. Mathews push the car around the corner back to his house. Mr. Mathews had been an auto mechanic in the Army and said he would make the repairs himself. Dad looked dubious. As we drove home, Dad remarked that he would be surprised if the frame wasn't bent and how lucky it was that no one had been killed.

That June there was a story in the newspaper stating that, due to budget cuts all the afterschool programs at the middle school from art to athletics, were axed. I was crushed, as I had finished the 7th grade with two letters (football and track) and planned to letter again at least two more times to beat Suzy's middle school record. I didn't know what I would do without afterschool sports.

In August, as if in answer to a prayer, Suzy invited me to a field hockey camp the high school was holding. It was an experiment to see if the high school programs could accommodate the extra kids to make up for the loss of sports at the middle schools. Mom really liked Suzy and was trying to make peace with the Mathews family, so she let me go.

On Monday morning I rode my bike to the high school dressed in my soccer clothes per Suzy's instructions and carrying a backpack with my water bottle. I had never played field hockey before, but if Suzy played it, it had to be fun.

Suzy was a senior now and played forward for the Wilson High School Wildcats. In the summer the team practiced twice a day on a field next to the football stadium. The first practice was from 7:00 to 9:30 in the morning, the second one was from 2 to 4:30 in the afternoon. I arrived ten minutes early because Dad taught me if you weren't at least five minutes early, you were late.

I parked my 10-speed next to the metal bleachers. There

were several other bicycles parked there that belonged to the players. There were twenty-five girls in all, sitting on the ground and stretching. Four grown women, who I (correctly) presumed to be the coaches stood off to the side, clipboards in hand.

The four coaches all looked like typical women PE teachers—kind of muscular, kind of stern, and seriously in charge. All of them wore black shorts and gold polo shirts and whistles on lanyards around their necks and gold sun visors to shade their eyes. Field hockey was serious business at Wilson High. The school had produced no fewer than five Olympians in the last fifteen years. The girls wore practice uniforms consisting of black cleats, black shorts, white tube socks and a gold tank top with a cartoon of Rosie the Wildcat, the Wilson High mascot carrying a field hockey stick and walking with purpose. Their game uniforms consisted of black trunks and a traditional kilt in a gold and black tartan. On top they wore short-sleeved gold V-neck jerseys with the player's last name and team number on them.

Coach Carol Norton was in charge. She had been at the high school for years and everyone loved her. She greeted me warmly. "Are you one of our middle school newbies?" she asked as I dropped my backpack on the lowest step of the bleachers.

"Yes, ma'am."

Suzy, who was sitting on the ground stretching, sprang to her feet to introduce me.

"This is Morgan Flynn, I told you about her," Suzy said, looking at all four coaches, but especially at Coach Norton, because she was the one who decided who played and what position.

"What position do you play?" asked the shortest coach. Her name was Terry Jerra. She had been a field medic in the Army, and when she wasn't coaching she taught biology.

"I don't know – I've never played before," I shrugged.

The coaches shared a look, and Suzy smiled impishly as she said slowly and deliberately, "Put her in the goal."

"The goal!" the big blonde coach exclaimed. Her name was Joyce Anderson, Ms. Anderson when she wasn't on the field. The varsity girls called her the Viking Queen. She taught creative writing and coached defense because she had played sweeper and goalie for the United States Marine Corps field hockey team. "Seriously?" she sputtered, giving Suzy a look. "She looks a little... small for that."

I bristled. "I play goalie in soccer!"

"Don't let her size fool you," Suzy went on like I wasn't even there. "She's tough. In the first grade she was jumped by three bigger girls. She sent them all to the hospital."

"Suzy!" I exclaimed, embarrassed and horrified that she would tell that story and, worse yet exaggerate it.

"She also plays football, lettered in at Hoover," Suzy continued. "Nobody got near the quarterback when Morgan was on the job. She's so badass they had her play with the eighth graders when she was in the seventh grade."

"Jesus, Suzy," I winced. Suzy later explained she had heard that from her mother, who apparently got this information from my mother. The truth was I was made to play with the eighth graders because I was heavy – I was five feet tall and weighed

150 pounds. My mother did not like the fact I was made to play with the larger girls. She said I was heavy as a choice, and it was to punish her and embarrass Laura. I didn't understand how my body was about them.

Coach Anderson looked at Coach Norton, who shrugged then nodded her approval. "Okay, we'll try her in the goal."

"Yes!" Suzy grinned.

I threw Suzy a slightly annoyed look.

Four more girls from the middle school showed up. All four of them had older sisters on the team. One of them was Julie Korn whose sister Mary played on varsity. I was glad she was late and missed Suzy's story about the three girls I sent to the hospital since she had been one of them. I didn't relish the idea of playing on a team with her because Julie and her cronies still picked on me occasionally. Julie resented the fact I was in the smart classes.

The morning began with warm up laps then Coach Norton fitted the new players for sticks. The stick was sized off your height— it had to come up to your hip bone. My stick was only 32 inches. I quickly realized I was the shortest player on the field.

As I was walking toward the goal, Julie, who was now a good three inches taller than me, tripped me with her newly issued stick and called me a "short, fat, klutz" when I fell down. I sprang to my feet and launched myself into Julie like a tackle in football. I wanted to let her—and everyone else on the team—know that I was not going to put up with that kind of crap. Julie looked surprised when I knocked her on her butt then grabbed her by the front of her shirt and suggested she watch what she did with her stick or else I'd shove it up her ass. Everybody was surprised—even me.

The coaches looked at each other and I thought for sure they would send me home or at least assign me penalty laps, but instead they just sort of bit back smiles as Suzy, standing there announced smugly, "Told ya! The girl was born to play defense!"

Mary Korn scowled and shook her head at her sister.

"No more horseplay, you two," Coach Norton scolded, looking at Julie and then me. "You guys are on the same team now."

"Let's see if she's a hockey goalie," Coach Anderson said, taking me to the area behind the goal cage where I would suit up in the protective gear of a goalkeeper. The goalies wore padded gear over their feet called kickers, leg guards and a glove on one hand. In the other hand, they would carry their sticks. The goalkeeper is the only player allowed to touch the ball with something other than their stick. When the ball came toward the goal, the goalie rushed out of the cage and blocked the ball, kicking it away with her feet. There were three other goalies already in their gear. Two played on the junior varsity and the biggest goalie, Linda, was the varsity goalie.

Linda was a senior. She wore a rolled up bandana to keep her dark hair out of her face. Even if she had been dressed in a prom gown she would still look like a goalie. She was a good eight inches taller than me with a stocky build. "You're gonna play goalie?" she asked, looking me up and down incredulously. "How old are you?"

"Thirteen going on fourteen and yes, I want to play goalie. You got a problem with that?"

Linda started to laugh. "Good attitude! What you lack in size you make up in spunk! Okay, Spunky, let's see what we can do with you!"

Linda demonstrated how goalkeepers held their sticks. It was different from field players who kept their sticks down low to dribble, pass and block, only the flat side of the stick could be used.

Linda and Coach Anderson showed me how to put on the protective gear. The goalie pads were sort of a canvas and cotton batting around bamboo. Leather straps held the gear in place, and I felt like Godzilla as I tried to move in it. Linda assured me that I would get the hang of it, then showed me how to scuttle sideways like a crab.

"Footwork is everything for a goalie," she said. "Stay on your toes!"

The goal cage for field hockey is a lot smaller than the goal for soccer. Linda demonstrated various blocking techniques. She then took shots at me so I could practice what I had learned. I was having a marvelous time!

After a water break Coach Norton called for a scrimmage. Half the girls put black t-shirts over their practice uniforms so we would know who was on which teams. Because there were four goalies, we took turns in each cage. I shared the cage with Linda. When I wasn't in the cage, I stood behind it, watching Linda. When I was in the cage, Linda and Coach Anderson stood behind me telling me what to do.

When I blocked a shot, kicking the ball off to the side like I saw Linda do, Coach Anderson shouted, "By George, I think she's got it!"

Suzy was on the opposing team. She had been playing hockey since her freshman year and it showed. She wasn't the tallest girl on the team, but she sure was one of the fastest. I watched her as she sprinted down the field, a look of determination on her face. I couldn't get over how her body had changed since the last time I saw her in June. Her waist had diminished, and she had hips and boobs now, but they didn't get in the way. I was surprised and embarrassed when I realized that my childhood friend had morphed into a woman. I still hadn't quite made it yet. I had broad shoulders and starter boobs but was missing hips and a waist.

The offense was moving toward the goal. It was three girls; Suzy was one of them. She called to her teammates to pass to her.

"Stay on your toes, follow the ball!" Linda coached from behind the cage. "Stay with it!"

I stood in a goalie's crouch, keeping on my toes as I moved sideways, protecting the goal. Suzy had the ball. She dodged and weaved, and then I somewhat awkwardly charged out of the goal, trying to get the ball, but instead I collided with Suzy. With a loud WOOF! Suzy tumbled over me, falling forward but not letting go of her stick. She did an incredible somersault and landed on her feet, while I tripped over my own feet and went down face first. Whistles blew as I lay face-down in the grass.

I groaned as I pushed myself up onto my elbows, and then to my knees.

"You okay kid?" Coach Anderson was on one knee next to me. "Can you get up?" I had big scrapes on both elbows and grass stains on my t-shirt.

"Are you hurt?" Coach Norton asked.

I shook my head. "I'm okay, I can walk it off," I said, although I smarted upwards of five places.

I got to my feet with the help of Coach Norton and started to walk somewhat unsteadily toward the sidelines behind the cage.

Suzy nodded her approval. "I taught her that," she said, beaming with pride as she shouted "Rub some dirt on it!" making the other girls laugh.

Coach Anderson waved Linda into the goal.

"Good job, Spunky," Linda said, tapping my stick with hers as she jogged on to the field. The whistle blew to call the game back into play.

CHAPTER 6

Junior Wildcat

When the school year started middle schoolers were allowed to attend practices on Monday, Wednesday, and Friday, but weren't allowed to play in the games which were on Tuesdays and Thursdays. On Friday the coaches divided the team for scrimmages. Each girl had the chance to play a different position. I only wanted to play goalie. It allowed me to be physically aggressive without getting into trouble. I needed that outlet. I had a bad temper. I got angry a lot, usually at Laura who was always stealing from me or trying to get me into trouble by telling my mother lies about me or blaming me when she did something. Even when Laura hit me I wasn't allowed to hit back because Laura, according to Mom, had 'so many problems'. Field hockey, I decided, was a safety valve for me.

Suzy knew things weren't so great at home for me, so she took me under her wing. We practiced together on the weekends in her front yard using a goal made from two lawn chairs. She taught me the Wildcat growl (something the team did before each game or when they scored) and one time I slept over and we watched *The Wizard of Oz*. It was her favorite movie. She told me when she was little she used to hide behind Rick when the Wicked Witch of the West appeared. I was surprised to hear that, since I didn't think Suzy had ever been afraid of anything.

One thing I didn't like about field hockey was that we had to shower after practice. As each girl came into the locker room they handed off their equipment to Coach Anderson, then Coach Jerra handed each girl a clean towel. The towels were white and a little smaller than a bath sheet. You could wrap yourself in it, covering yourself from your chest to mid-thigh if you weren't too tall. The communal showers were located at the end of the locker rows. I was shy around the older girls, so I showered quickly. Suzy timed me more than once and said I averaged three minutes. I had to be fast in the mornings, I said, because Laura was such a bathroom hog. Suzy liked longer showers, sometimes staying under the water for a full ten minutes.

I attended the home games. Because of the time my school got out I missed most of the varsity game -- I made it for the last twenty minutes -- but I was able to watch the junior varsity game in its entirety. Usually there were just a handful of spectators on the bleachers. One girl was always there. Her name was Winnifred, she had been on the junior varsity team the year before. Winifred had shoulder-length red hair with bangs and always wore slacks and a button-down shirt or a Fair Isle sweater and a pearl choker like June Cleaver. Over all of this, she wore a long black raincoat covered with buttons advertising British punk bands. She radiated sophistication. Winnifred always sat on the top row of the bleachers. She appeared to be doing her homework, looking up only when the offense had the ball. I wondered why she was at the games at all, then someone told me she was from Scotland where field hockey was really big, so I guessed she was there because she was homesick. The only reason I knew her name was because I overheard Coach Anderson talking to her about a homework assignment. Apparently, Winnifred wrote poetry and had even been published. Coach Anderson wanted her to enter a literary contest. That got my interest, because I had been writing short stories and novels since the first grade — but I never shared them with anyone outside of turning in a few stories in as creative writing assignments in English class. I wanted to be published someday. I didn't think I was good enough yet. And I was afraid to find out.

One day Winnifred was carrying a black guitar case. It was the last home game of the season. The winner of the game advanced to the regional finals. The varsity game went into overtime because it was tied 1-1. Winnifred was apparently not happy about the extension of the game, because she made a face, then took the guitar out and started to play. The guitar was a steel-string like the one I had at home.

Winnifred saw me watching her. "Do you play guitar?" she asked.

"Yes," I replied.

"What kind of music?"

"Oldies mostly," I replied. "Doo-wop and Beatles."

"Oh. I play classical," she said, her fingers flew across the fretboard, both impressing and intimidating me. "I play several instruments: guitar, flute, piano and harp. I write music."

"That's cool," I said. "My name is Morgan."

"I know," Winnifred replied as she played a Spanish classical piece.

Before I could ask how she knew my name, there was a roar from the field that got our attention. Suzy was charging the opposition's goal, the ball in her possession. Deanna, who played wing, and Bonnie, who played midfield, were running with her. The opposing team tried to stop Suzy, who passed the ball to Bonnie on the right, who was just outside of the defense circle. You had to shoot from inside the circle for the goals to count. The goalie focused on Bonnie, who was in possession of the ball. Bonnie passed the ball to Deanna, drawing the goalie's attention. Suzy slipped behind the goalie, calling for the pass. Deanna was strong and quick, and sent the ball toward Suzy. As both the sweeper's and goalie's attention shifted, Suzy whirled around and passed the ball back to Bonnie, who, now inside the circle and unguarded, drove the ball into the left corner of the goal cage. The goalie lunged but missed — score one for the Wildcats!

The referee blew the whistle indicating the end of the game. A huge roar went up from the field and from the sidelines. Suzy, Bonnie, and Deanna jumped into each other's arms and the rest of the team swarmed them, all of them growling. The Wildcats would advance to the regional finals!

I jumped to my feet applauding and doing the Wildcat growl. I couldn't wait to get to high school and be part of that scene.

CHAPTER 7

Suck it up, Buttercup

"*S*punky! Glad to see you back!" Linda, the goalie-turned coach, greeted me the first day of practice of my freshman year. Both Linda and Suzy were freshmen at the local community college. They had scholarships for field hockey and both had been hired as part-time coaches for the Wildcats.

I was fourteen now and had my first boyfriend, Kevin. We started dating that summer. Kevin had dark hair and eyes and, like many other guys his age, a mouth full of metal. He was skinny and tall and ran cross-country for Wilson. They practiced twice a day, just like the field hockey team did. Over the summer we went to the movies a few times and he came over to swim. Kevin seemed most interested in the pool and trying to get into my pants. I wasn't ready for that and told him so. My mother liked him because he was on the honor roll and she said he was 'good' for me.

On the first day of practice, Suzy and Deanna, who was a senior now, greeted the new players and showed them how to pass and trap balls with their sticks. Then Suzy told the returning players to warm up with passes. The older girls all got these impish looks on their faces and then started shooting en masse, sending the balls toward Suzy, who danced and jumped to avoid being hit and blocked as many shots as she could, yelling "Quit it, ya bunch of weasels!"

"Dance, Mathews, dance!" Linda yelled, laughing at her friend. Suzy was making noises of protest and laughing as she sprinted behind the goal cage for protection.

The behavior of the older girls puzzled me. I looked at Coach Norton.

"Do they not like Suzy or something?" I asked.

Coach Norton was trying hard not to laugh. "That's not it," she chuckled with a dismissive wave of her hand. "I'll explain it to you when you're older."

"Yes, ma'am," I said as I started putting on the gear. I hadn't grown much that summer: five-feet-and-two-inches was all I was ever going to get in life, so I knew I would have to be fearless in the cage.

Suzy enjoyed her coaching job, saying it was the most fun job she had, and she had several. She said the sports scholarship would only go so far, so she was always looking for work. A week after she turned eighteen my parents hired her as a chaperone for Laura and I when they went out of town. She would be our legal guardian for two and a half days for the princely sum of $250. Laura, who was sixteen, resented Suzy being in charge, so much so that when Suzy was in the shower Saturday morning she said she was going to steal Suzy's bra with the intention of freezing it.

"Don't do it! She'll kill you!" I admonished Laura. I'd just as soon tickle a grizzly bear than mess with Suzy.

Laura ignored me and charged into the den where Suzy's clothes were neatly laid out on the arm of the couch she'd been sleeping on. The bra, a tasteful pink number with lace on the cups, was in plain sight. Laura picked it up by the clasp like she was holding a fish by the gills. "Jeez! She's tiny!" Laura exclaimed, reading the size tag. At sixteen Laura was already a C-cup. She let out a snort. "I think your boobs are bigger than hers?"

"Leave my boobs out of this!" I said crossly.

Laura ran into the kitchen waving the bra like a flag. She ran it under the faucet to wet it down, then shoved it in the freezer, hiding it under packages of frozen food. It was obvious Laura had done this before.

We returned to our places at the breakfast table. A few minutes later the shower stopped and Suzy, dressed in a blue bathrobe with her long dark hair hanging in wet quills down her back, came into the kitchen. She had an amused smirk on her face as she approached the table.

Suzy stood there with her hands on her hips as she sort of sized us up, trying to determine which one had done the deed. Finally, she spoke. "All right you guys -- where's my bra?"

I choked on a mouthful of waffle as Laura squeaked "What bra?"

Suzy's eyes narrowed. "My bra," she replied. "Come on you guys, jokes' over. Where's my bra?"

"In the freezer." Laura chirped helpfully.

Suzy's eyes went wide and became hard as flint, and I swear she got taller as she bellowed "WHAT? MY BRA IS WHERE?" She stormed over to the freezer and jerked the door open. Suzy was swearing blue and green as she dug her brassiere out from under the popsicles and packages of ground beef. She whipped around, holding the bra like it was edged weaponry, pointing it at Laura as she yelled, "Damn it, Laura! Stay away from my bra!"

I was reasonably certain this was a phrase Suzy had not antici-pated using that weekend in a house full of girls. Later, that night as we were making dinner — Laura had been banished to her room— Suzy gave me a look as she warned me not to tell anyone on the field hockey team that Laura had frozen her bra or that it was pink.

"I won't," I promised, feeling as if she was revealing her Kryp-tonite to me.

I wondered if a pink bra was in my future as Mom thought Suzy the epitome of the perfect daughter. Mom always held Suzy up as a role model. I should take the same classes, wear the same clothes, etc. Mom said Suzy was going to go far, unlike Laura, who according to my mother, was lazy and had better marry rich, or me, because, according to her, I screwed up intentionally and was a disappointment because I didn't live up to my potential. I was smart enough to get straight As, Mom said, and when I didn't, it was because I was lazy and wanted to hurt her. I didn't agree with that at all, and I didn't tell Suzy what Mom said, although it made me wonder if Suzy was disappointed in me too, as Mom made it sound like she consulted with Suzy on a regular basis.

That first semester Suzy was taking all general education classes as she hadn't decided on a major yet, although she talked about aerospace engineering or biology as possibilities. Both would mean transferring to a four-year school. Her father was against this, as he wanted her to become an urban planner like he was. Her mother wanted her to be an attorney, because that was what she wanted to be before she met Mr. Mathews and 'settled down'.

Suzy's college plans started a fight between our dads. One night when they had one of their Gourmet Group dinners at our house the after-dinner discussion turned to what the kids were doing. Dad said going to college without a clear plan was a waste of time and money. Mr. Mathews took offense, saying Suzy was wise to take advantage of the scholarship she'd been given in exchange for playing field hockey. He added that at least she had an idea of what she wanted to do, which was more than what could be said for Laura, who he knew was in a few remedial classes with Butch.

I was upstairs in my room working on a story when I heard their voices rising and Dad called for me to come downstairs. I thought this odd, since when the Gourmet Group met at our house we were supposed to be scarce. When I came into the living room I noticed that Mom and Mrs. Mathews looked upset. The other two couples looked uncomfortable. Mr. Mathews looked like he was spoiling for a fight. Dad looked smug.

"Morgan, what do you plan to study in college?" Dad asked calmly.

"Writing," I said, thinking it was a weird question. My parents had known for years that I wanted to be a writer.

"What kind of writing?" Mr. Mathews asked. "Like books?"

"Journalism," I said. "I plan to work for a daily newspaper or maybe a news magazine."

Dad looked at Mr. Mathews as if to say, "See? I told you so."

Mrs. Mathews looked at her husband and then sort of cleared her throat then asked me timidly, "How long have you known that you wanted to be a writer?"

"Since I was six."

"Six?" Mr. Mathews repeated, staring at me like he couldn't believe it.

"Yes, sir, in the first grade."

Mom looked proud as she said, "Morgan has been serious about writing for quite some time now. Last year for Christmas we gave her a dictionary, a big pack of black pens, a ream of binder paper, and a carton of correction fluid."

"I write every chance I get," I said helpfully. "I wrote my first novel when I was nine." I gestured over my shoulder. "I was just upstairs working on some science fiction. I'm trying to create strong female characters because there really aren't very many in popular literature — except for Princess Leia from *Star Wars.*" That made them all chuckle. Dad, looking very pleased, excused me with a wave.

Little did I know how much trouble he had created for me.

The moment I arrived at practice the following Monday Suzy ordered me into the goal cage.

"Shouldn't I run a lap first to warm up?" I asked. Coach Anderson had warned us that goalies got hurt if they didn't warm up before they got into the cage.

"This is the warm-up," Suzy said brusquely. "Into the goal, let's go,"

"Okay," I said, wondering why Suzy was working with me since she usually worked with the offense.

Suzy, dressed in her coach's uniform, walked to the top of the defense circle, her stick in her right hand, a mesh bag of hockey balls in her left hand. She dumped the balls out and lined them up so that they were parallel to the goal cage and about two feet apart. There were ten in all.

She paused at the first ball. "Ya ready?" she held her stick poised to strike.

I dropped into the goalie stance. "Fire away!" I said.

That was a poor choice of words on my part, because Suzy whacked the first ball so hard it came off the pitch and hit my abdomen where I didn't have any protection.

"Ow!" I yelped, surprised at how much it stung. "Take it easy!"

The look Suzy gave me was pure evil as she yelled, "Suck it up, buttercup!"

She started hitting the balls in rapid succession. Fast and hard, they flew at me. She was lifting all of them. I blocked a few, but more bounced off me often where the pads didn't cover. It seemed to me that Suzy wasn't trying to score as much as she was trying to hit me. One got me on my right leg just above the pads. It hurt so bad I dropped to my knees, crying out in pain.

"On your feet, Morgan!" Suzy bellowed. "If you're gonna be a goalie you've got to be tough! Come on Flynn, on your feet!" Suzy launched another round of balls in rapid succession. There were more body shots and one bounced and caught me in the face. It stunned me and I hit the deck.

"You call that goalkeeping?" Suzy snarled. "Come on, Spunky! Show some effort! You wanna be a Wildcat? You've got to earn it!"

A chorus of whistles sounded as all the other coaches swarmed the circle, looks of disbelief and anger on their faces.

Linda grabbed Suzy by the shoulder and shook her. "What the hell are you doing?" she demanded.

"Warming up the goalie!" Suzy replied, breathing hard and her eyes snapping.

"Suzy, that was too much!" Coach Norton scowled. "She doesn't have the skill or experience for that yet!" She glared at Suzy as if Suzy should have known better.

Coaches Jerra and Anderson came up on either side of me and helped me to my feet. Coach Anderson tilted my head up. "Let's see your face,"

"It got me between the eyes," I said, blinking. "I think I'm okay?"

"No, you're not," Coach Jerra stepped back, looking disgusted. "Your nose is bleeding,"

I looked down. There was a fair amount of blood on my gold t-shirt.

Coach Norton ordered Coaches Anderson and Jerra to take me to the training room and check me for more injuries. Coach Jerra was in full medic mode, asking me what hurt the worst.

"What the hell was Suzy doing?" Coach Anderson muttered, throwing an angry look over her shoulder.

"I think she was trying to kill me," I muttered, glancing at Suzy. Coach Norton had pulled Suzy to the sidelines and was standing over her, her hands on her hips as she talked to her. Suzy had her arms folded on her chest, her head bowed, and her eyes closed tight. She was obviously getting a talking-to.

In the team room they had me take off the gear and sit on the training table while they examined me. Coach Jerra handed me an ice pack to put on the bridge of my nose and they put a damp cloth on the back of my neck to help my nose stop bleeding. More ice packs were deployed. I had a purple and black bruise on the inside of my left arm on my bicep and another just below my elbow. The worst one was a red and purple bruise the size of a softball on my right thigh. Coach Jerra wanted me to take off my clothes so she could check the rest of me, but I protested modestly and refused.

"I'm Catholic, I can't take my clothes off unless I'm showering or it's my wedding night, and I am going to have to be really, really drunk for that." I squeaked.

They both sort of smirked and Coach Jerra sighed, "Okay, okay, understood," she reached for the ice pack on my face. "Let's see the nose."

They both winced when they saw the bruise. Coach Jerra didn't think my nose was broken, but said I might get two black eyes from the impact.

"Wonderful," I groused, wondering what my mother would say or if she would believe me when I told her Suzy had been the one that hit me.

"We'll see about getting you a helmet," said Coach Anderson briskly. "And body armor like the college girls wear. You've got a more physical style than the other goalies. At the very least you need to start wearing a mouthguard."

Coach Norton came into the team room with a contrite Suzy in tow. "How bad?" Coach Norton looked at Coach Jerra.

"A few contusions and a little blood from the nose, but nothing broken," Coach Jerra replied, "bruise between the eyes, the left arm, right leg and we think a few under the clothes," She threw a look at Suzy as she demanded "Just what were you trying to do?"

"Warm her up," Suzy replied defensively, the color rising in her face. "She was wearing the gear!"

Coach Anderson scowled as she reached over, pushing up the leg of my shorts so the large bruise on my thigh was more visible. "The pads don't cover everything," she said, giving Suzy a sharp look.

"It's part of the game!" Suzy stammered, but I could tell she was upset. She looked at me. "I'm sorry, Morgan, I guess I got carried away." There were tears in her eyes.

"It's okay," I said. "I'm a tomboy, we're supposed to be tough."

A flicker of recognition registered in Suzy's eyes. "Right," a smile tugged at the corner of her mouth.

"I'm sorry Coach," I said, looking at Coach Norton. "I wasn't able to stop very many. I'll work on that," I said miserably.

Coach Norton rolled her eyes and addressed the ceiling – this was something she did when she was close to losing her temper, then she looked at me. "Do you want to be a red shirt today? Do you want to sit out this practice?"

"No, ma'am," I shook my head. "I want to play."

"Okay," she nodded. "Just take it easy, okay? If you start to hurt too much, you step out, okay?"

"Yes, ma'am," I hopped off the table and started to put the gear back on. I was in pain and trying to hide it, but I don't think I did a very good job of it.

Coach Norton nodded to Coach Anderson. "See that she's warmed up properly. Jerra, please start with the passing drills for the forwards. Suzy, give me a hand with the water jug for the girls." In the mirror, I saw the color drain from Suzy's face. 'Give me a hand with the water jug' was Coach Norton-speak for "I AM GOING TO TEAR YOU A NEW ONE."

My teammates applauded and did the Wildcat growl when I returned to the field. Suzy and Coach Norton joined us a few minutes later, hauling the large water jug and the paper cups. Suzy looked like she had been crying.

We started the traditional end of practice scrimmage. Suzy and Linda were acting both as players and as referees, carrying their sticks and running up and down the field with their whistles in their mouths. As the offense descended on the goal I came out of the cage just like I had been taught to and collided with a forward. We both lost our balance. Instinctively I threw an arm out trying to catch her but we went down in a heap. Whistles blew, signaling misconduct.

"Red card!" Suzy barked, pointing at me. "Morgan, you pull that kind of crap in a game, and you're going to get a red card. You could cost us the game! What is wrong with you?"

I was stunned as I got to my knees. I looked at the forward laying on her side next to me. Her name was Karen, and I knew her from grade school. She was a sophomore who wore her long blonde hair in braids that made her look like she should be on a can of instant hot chocolate.

"I'm sorry," I said automatically. "Are you hurt? Did I hurt you?"

"No," Karen shook her head as she checked herself for injuries. She sat up. "I don't think so. I think I ran into you?" she said, throwing a confused look at Suzy.

I nodded, then looked at Suzy. "What did I do wrong?" I asked.

"You tackled another player!" Suzy shouted. "You don't physically tackle the other players! This isn't football!"

"I didn't mean to! I lost my balance," I sputtered, surprised at her hostility.

"You don't tackle the other players!" Suzy repeated. "Do you hear me?"

"Yeah. Do you hear me?" I shot back my anger rising to match hers.

"Lose the attitude," Suzy snarled.

"Right back at you," I said, getting to my feet. I didn't like her yelling at me in front of everyone.

"That's enough ladies," Coach Jerra warned, walking onto the pitch and looking from Suzy to me and back to Suzy again. The rest of the team sort of hung back and looked uncomfortable.

Suzy shook her head slowly and took a few steps away from me, then she looked back as she said, "Morgan, maybe you don't have the maturity for this? Maybe you shouldn't be playing?"

Her words stung and then I proved my lack of maturity when I said, "Maybe it should have been you instead of Rick?" I swear to God I don't know where that came from. My voice was flat and vicious, and the words were out of my mouth before my brain realized what I had said. It surprised both of us. I had no idea I could be so ugly, but I guess I was still angry with her for hurting me.

Suzy sort of gasped and stumbled back, all the color going out of her face. Her eyes narrowed as she hissed "You little fuck!" She dropped her stick and lunged at me.

I dropped my stick and raised my fists to defend myself.

Linda, who was larger than Suzy by about three inches and twenty pounds grabbed Suzy around the waist, picking her up baby-tantrum style, and ran up field hauling Suzy like she was a sack of wheat, yelling as she did so, "No! No! No! Stop it! Stop it! She's a kid!"

"Put me down!" Suzy bellowed, arms and legs flailing. She hurled insults and threats at me. I yelled back something to the effect of "Bring it on!" and was tackled by half of the junior varsity.

"Stop it!" Coach Jerra shouted. "Both of you!"

"Look out!"

I looked up to see Suzy had broken away from Linda and was charging toward me. Linda was sort of staggering, because Suzy had hit her in the face with her flailing.

Coach Anderson came off the sidelines and tackled Suzy like a linebacker, yelling at her to calm down. She put Suzy into a full-wrestling hold and held her pinned to the ground facedown. Suzy kicked wildly, trying to break free.

Coach Norton was furious. She came off the sidelines blowing her whistle and shaking her head as if she could not believe what she was seeing. She was glaring daggers as she addressed the team.

"Ladies – showers." Then she fixed her gaze on me and said through clenched teeth, "Morgan, fifteen laps with the gear on, backwards."

"Yes, ma'am!" I said and took off running. I was ashamed of myself, embarrassed and horrified by what I had said. Fifteen laps the regular way was a long way to run without gear on. With all the gear and backwards it would seem even longer.

Coach Norton stepped in front of a still squirming Suzy. "Mathews, we need to talk," her voice was full of danger.

Suzy stopped squirming and looked scared as Coach Anderson helped her to her feet. "Carol, be careful," Coach Anderson warned, still holding Suzy by the arms. Suzy looked terrified as a seething Coach Norton grabbed her under the chin and pulled her face up so she was looking her in the eye. I caught the words "don't you ever" and "we do not" before I was out of ear shot. When I came around for the second lap Coach Norton and Coach Anderson were on either side of Suzy and the three of them were walking toward the track. Suzy had her head bowed and her arms folded on her chest.

I felt terrible about what I said and started to cry as I plodded along. The straps for the gear chafed me and I felt raw spots forming on the backs of my knees. By lap five I was limping, my legs felt like lead, and my throat was on fire.

It was about lap eight when Coach Anderson appeared at the top of the field. "Time to come in, Morgan," she called to me. She didn't look angry anymore.

"I can't," I cried. "I'm only on the eighth lap? I have seven more to go."

Coach Anderson gave me a look. "I don't think you're going to make it to fifteen, you look pretty beat."

"I need to finish these laps," I bawled. "I don't want Coach Norton to get any angrier with me, and I really owe it to Suzy for what I said," I said, jogging in place. I was worried that if I stopped moving I wouldn't be able to start again. "Please let me finish?"

Coach Anderson sighed. "No, it's okay, Morgan, Coach Norton sent me out here to get you. It's time to hit the showers."

I fell into step next to her, limping and staggering a bit. I started to cry so hard I had to stop walking.

"I don't know what I did!" I wailed.

"Did you two have some sort of fight recently?"Coach Anderson gave me a look.

"I don't think so," I shook my head. "When I got to practice today she told me to get in the cage then she started shooting at me like she wanted to hit me on purpose. I think she is trying to toughen me up," my voice trembled as I asked, "Am I that bad?"

"No, no, you're right where you should be," Coach Anderson said, gently placing a hand on my shoulder. "You're still learning the game."

"Please don't kick me off the team!" I cried.

"That's really up to Coach Norton," she gave me a scolding look. "She's not really happy with either one of you right now."

"Yes, ma'am, I don't blame her," I sniffed glumly as we resumed our walk. "I'm not happy with us either."

That made Coach Anderson smile.

I was the last one back in. I was moving slowly, and Coach Jerra winced when she saw me. I turned in my gear and picked up my towel and then went to my locker to deposit my clothes.

The door to the coach's office was closed. I had a feeling Suzy was there.

I was in the showers with my back to the locker room when I heard someone approaching behind me. I glanced over my shoulder to see Suzy, buck naked heading for the showers. She acted like she didn't see me. She hung her towel on a hook, then went to the nozzle at the far end of the row. She stood under the spray facing the wall, her eyes closed. She was grinding her teeth and shaking her head slowly as the water blasted her face.

The sound of someone slamming a locker followed by a second slam got our attention, and we both looked over our shoulders. Coach Norton, using her pass key, had opened both our lockers and grabbed all our clothes. Coach Jerra, Anderson and Linda were standing next to her. Coach Norton handed our clothes to them, and all four stood there, glaring at us in the showers.

Embarrassed, I stepped out of the spray and grabbed my towel to cover up.

"What's going on?" I yelped.

Suzy, the color rising in her face, grabbed her towel and covered up as well.

Coach Norton folded her arms on her chest. "Morgan? Suzy? We had a meeting of the coaching staff. We decided that your behavior is against the grace of the game. We're wondering if you two should be allowed to continue."

Suzy and I looked at each other.

Coach Norton continued, "It appears that Suzy shouldn't be a coach because she seems to have a problem controlling her temper, and it appears you, Morgan, also have trouble controlling your temper. Perhaps we should yard both of you?"

"Yard?" I repeated, unsure of what the term meant.

"Kick us off the team," Suzy said. She started to tear up as she addressed the coaches who were nodding in agreement. "No! Please – I need this job!"

"Don't fire her!" I cried, glancing at Suzy. "I'll quit if you want me to, but don't fire Suzy! She loves this game too much, and it wouldn't be fair to the other girls to deprive them of her experience!"

This was quite an eloquent speech, especially considering I was pretty much in my birthday suit.

The coaches exchanged a look and there was a pause, with the only noise being the sound of the water running. Coach Norton sighed, then looking at the ceiling she asked, "Am I discerning a personal problem here?"

I had no idea what that meant, but apparently Suzy did, because she swallowed hard and answered, "Well, yes."

"Resolve it!" Coach Norton bellowed so loud we both flinched. She glared at us as she said, "I'm giving you five minutes to talk this out and make peace or else your clothes are staying here and you two are going home in those towels."

"What?" I squeaked, not believing what I had just heard.

Coach Norton repeated the ultimatum. The other coaches looked angry — except for Linda, who, black eye and all, sort of smirked, looking skyward as if she found a spot on the ceiling that commanded her attention. She was shaking with suppressed laughter.

Suzy reached around quickly to turn off the water.

"Please don't do this," she begged.

"Five minutes!" Coach Norton bellowed and marched back to the office, the others in tow.

I held my towel tight and my hand was shaking as I turned off my shower. They had all our clothes — street clothes, uniforms, even our shoes!

"She wouldn't really make us go home in towels, would she?" I whimpered.

"Yes, she would," Suzy's face was ashen, as apparently she had seen this form of discipline before.

I knew I did not want to walk nine blocks in nothing but a towel.

"I'm so sorry for what I said about Rick," I started to cry. "Please forgive me. It was horrible! I don't know where that came from?"

Suzy glared at me. "Where it came from is that you wanted to hurt me. And you did!"

"You hurt me first! You didn't even let me warm up! You weren't trying to score, you were trying to injure me!" I howled, then gestured to the bruises as I added, "And you did! In spades!"

Suzy backed away from me as she snarled, "Bruises fade! What you said about Rick – "

"I know that was awful!" I interrupted her. "That was horrible and I'm sorry!" I shrank back and started shivering because the air conditioning in the locker room had been turned on. "I shouldn't have said it! But you hurt me first! You've been mad at me all day and I don't know what I did!" I lifted the towel slightly to expose more of the red and purple bruise on my right thigh. "What did I do to deserve this?" I was bawling now. "Please tell me why you are so angry with me that you want to physically hurt me?"

Suzy cringed and turned her face away. In a voice filled with tears she told me how angry her father had been when he came home from the Gourmet Group. "Your father was acting all high and mighty because you already know that you want to be a writer," she said in a high, pleading tone. "Apparently I'm crap because I don't have a career or a college major picked out yet."

"Good God, no!" I shook my head. "My parents don't think you're crap! They love you! My mother wishes you were her daughter!"

Suzy looked at me, surprised. "Really?"

"Absolutely! Mom said you're the kind of daughter she wanted. I think she even tried to adopt you once but she couldn't reach an agreement with your parents about how many goats you were worth!"

Suzy, who was also starting to shiver, started to laugh and cry at the same time. "You and that quick wit of yours! You are going to be a great writer someday," she said as she wiped her tears with the back of her hand.

"I don't understand why you took it out on me," I said plaintively. "It should have been my dad in the goal and my dad standing here in a towel!"

Suzy let out a bark of laughter. "And my dad in a towel in the girl's locker room! That would be a sight!" she hooted, rolling her eyes.

"I don't want to go home in a towel, and I don't want to be kicked off the team," I cried. "And I don't want them to fire you!"

"I'm sorry I hurt you," Suzy blubbered as she ran her eyes over the damage she had inflicted.

"I am sorry I hurt you with what I said about Rick," I replied. "Please forgive me?"

"I forgive you," Suzy sniffed. "Do you forgive me?"

"Yes."

Coach Norton's voice rang out from the office. "Thirty seconds, ladies! What's it gonna be? Have you made up yet? Or are you going home like that?"

Suzy looked at me. "Are we made up?"

"I think so," I replied through chattering teeth.

"We made up!" Suzy cried and I joined her yelling, "We made up!"

We were both shivering and cringing with embarrassment and humiliation when the coaches marched into the locker bank. Linda and Coach Jerra had our clothes. They were smirking and looking very proud of themselves. Later, Linda told me that the minute they entered the office they had switched on the AC to provide "extra incentive" for a quick resolution to the personal problem.

"I never want to hear about this day again," Coach Norton said, looking from me to Suzy. "And I never want to see that behavior out there again. From either one of you. Am I clear?"

"Yes, ma'am," we replied in unison.

"You are both on probation for the next month. Suzy, in addition to coaching you're going to be cleaning up sticks and be the water girl. Morgan, you will arrive at morning practice fifteen minutes early and will be running three extra laps with the gear on. If either one of you steps so much as one nano-millimeter out of line, you're gone. Understood ladies?"

"Yes, ma'am," we barked, and then Suzy who was so relieved that she wasn't going to get fired started to cry again and that set me off. We both stood there, shivering and crying and trying very hard to stop and not being terribly successful.

Coach Norton sort of looked at us, then her face relaxed and she gestured for the others to put our clothes down on the benches.

She sighed. "Normally I would make you hug, but since you're both naked, that doesn't seem appropriate."

"Thank you," I whimpered, and Suzy nodded in agreement.

The others laughed and Coach Norton smiled gently as she said, "Get your clothes on so you don't catch a cold, and go home. Let's have a better day tomorrow."

CHAPTER 8

Pressure Comes in Many Forms

$\mathcal{M}$y relationship changed with Suzy after that. I distanced myself from her, even addressing her as ma'am until one day when she told me to stop because it bothered her. I was surprised, since my Marine Corps father had taught me ma'am was a term of respect, and any woman over the age of eighteen was a ma'am.

Winnifred, the mysterious girl who used to watch field hockey games, was still in school, a senior now, but no longer came to the games. She did, however, watch practices. She sat on the slope above the field, often with her guitar or sometimes a flute, and played music. We joked about her writing *Flute Sonata to Run Laps By*. There were a few times when I saw Suzy glance up at Winnifred and smile shyly and wave. Winnifred always waved back.

One day Suzy was missing from practice. That night over dinner Mom told us that Butch Mathews had disappeared.

"The last time they saw him was Sunday afternoon, when he said he was going over to a friend's house — he hasn't been seen since," Mom explained, looking worried. "He took his bike with him. Mrs. Mathews called me today to tell me about it."

Mom added that it would kill the Mathews if they lost another child.

Laura suggested Butch was kidnapped, saying Butch hung out at the back gate of the high school where the drug dealers were said to be. The Back Gaters as those kids were known, were frequently stoned or drunk, and by their third or fourth year they were shipped off to the continuation school where all the high schools in the district dumped their problem children.

Mom gave Laura a sharp look. "Do you have any idea where he might be?"

"No, but Morgan probably does," Laura said, giving me a dirty look.

"Why would I know?" I was surprised.

"Kids talk about the bandana you wear when you play field hockey, just like the kids at the back gate wear. I've seen you at the back gate! You're probably smoking!" Laura said accusingly.

Mom looked so disappointed as she demanded, "Are you smoking?"

"No!" I was offended by the question. "I wear the bandanna to keep the hair out of my eyes!" I added that most of the girls on the team who had bangs did the same. "I don't hang out at the back gate!"

Laura started in, claiming she had seen me smoking at school. I vehemently denied it.

"Enough of this!" Dad snapped, glaring at Laura.

Laura continued like she hadn't heard him. "You're a freshman and freshmen will do anything to fit in, I wouldn't be surprised if you drank at school too."

"No, Laura, that's you," I replied sarcastically. "You're the one who broke into the liquor cabinet and got drunk with your friends and lit the carpet on fire,"

"You're so masculine!" Laura sneered at me. "When you wear the bandanna you look like a guy! You do it to shame the family! If you hate us so much, why don't you leave?"

"I would love to," I sighed. And I meant it.

Mom lost it at that point, screaming at me that I was grounded for a week for saying such a hateful thing. Dad countered that he was tired of Laura picking on me and trying to get me in trouble, and if I said I wasn't smoking or drinking he believed me. That started my parents arguing and Dad ordered us to our rooms.

"See what you did?" Laura hissed as we headed up the stairs. Laura told me that if our parents divorced it would be my fault. I didn't understand why Laura was upset about that, since she often talked about how much she hated Dad. Once she even asked me if I knew anyone who could kill him.

Laura didn't like me either. It started the day I was born. I was born eight weeks premature. I was in an incubator for a long time, and Mom was in the hospital for a long time with complications. Laura was a toddler but old enough to understand that my birth kept Mom in the hospital and away from her and she feared Mom would die. Laura resented me greatly for this. On this particular night she also accused me of being on steroids because something was making me so masculine. Mom must have heard her because that night Mom tore my room apart looking for cigarettes and steroids and God knows what else. She dumped out drawers, pulled the books off shelves and stripped the bed looking for contraband. This was not the first time she tossed my room. She had been doing it on a semi-regular basis since I entered my teens. She called it "showing concern". I called it "being a control freak." I learned not to fight back, because that would make it worse. I just stood there while she tore the place apart and wondered what I had done to make my mother hate me so.

Sometimes when she was angry she would intentionally damage my possessions. When I was eight, she smashed the model of a P-38 Lightning I built. Another time she stabbed my teddy bear in the chest with a kitchen knife because she said I was intentionally hurting her by not being the daughter she wanted. When I was twelve she smashed my first soccer trophy. She never did this kind of thing to Laura. I resented these searches, these invasions of privacy. Mom wouldn't even let us have locks on our bedroom doors, although she and Dad had one. Mom said we didn't need them.

Laura shared this lack of boundaries — she would walk into my room without knocking and help herself to whatever she wanted. For example, when I was in the first grade I won my first writing contest, and I won a giant-sized Hershey bar. I gave some chocolate to Laura and intended to save the rest of it to share with Dad. But when Dad got home and I went to get the chocolate bar, there was nothing but the wrapper left. Laura had eaten the whole thing, telling me she deserved more chocolate. I was in tears because I had very much wanted to share something I won with my father.

When Mom finished my room looked like a bomb had gone off in it. She hadn't found anything. "Feel better now?" I asked her.

Mom responded by slapping me across the face, knocking me sideways as she said, "Morgan Elizabeth Flynn! Don't you dare take that tone with me!"

Dad, who had been trying to get Mom to stop, let out a roar and jumped between us, telling Mom that if she touched me again, he would strike her. He told Mom that I was a good kid, and he didn't blame me for wanting to leave. Dad had left home as soon as he was able to, so I kind of figured it was genetic.

Laura who had been there egging Mom on screamed at Dad that if he tried to hit Mom, she would kill him. Dad responded by slapping Laura across the face, knocking her to the floor. Then Mom put up her hands as if to strike Dad and he grabbed her wrists, then sort of pushed her back and away from him, then stormed out of my room. Dad always left when he got angry, taking his truck for a drive until he calmed down. Laura ran after him, screaming that he shouldn't come back. Mom turned on me, telling me that I was responsible for Dad slapping Laura, and that Dad was probably going to commit suicide, and it would be my fault. Then she stormed out.

I closed my door and used my desk chair to block it, then set to putting my room back in order. It always made me sad when I did this. I wondered if it was normal for moms to terrorize their children, and wished I was old enough to leave and not come back. I didn't think Dad would kill himself. I figured that was wishful thinking on Mom's part. I wondered why Dad stayed with Mom. If I had been him, I would have left for good. Around midnight Dad came home — just like always.

The next day I left for school at 4:45 a.m., extra early because I just wanted to be out of the house. I intended to ride my bike to school, but my bike had two flat tires – Laura had punctured them because she was angry with me — she had done it several times before. I jogged to school. Coach Norton found me waiting outside the locker room when she arrived at 5:15 a.m. I was pacing back and forth in the dark trying to get warm.

"Morgan! What are you doing here so early?" she asked. She had her purse and gear bag over her shoulder and a cup of coffee in one hand. Practice began at 5:45 a.m. for me, 6:00 a.m. for the rest of the girls.

"Couldn't sleep, ma'am," I said, and I went straight to my locker to dress out.

Morning practice was all fundamentals and conditioning and was overseen by coaches Jerra, Anderson and Norton. Coach Anderson was pleased because the helmet she had ordered for me had come in. It was black with a silver face mask. She brought it out to me on the field. I was on the field in full gear running wind sprints when the rest of the team turned out in their gold sweatshirts. They all looked sleepy. I was wide-awake and pushing myself.

Practice was almost over when Laura showed up, marching right into the middle of a drill screaming at me that our parents were divorcing, it was my fault and if I hated the family so much I should just leave home or kill myself. Either was fine with her.

Coach Anderson went into Marine mode. "Who the hell are you?" she demanded and yelled at Laura to get off the field and to never attack one of her players again. Laura called her a dyke and asked if I was her lesbian lover. The defense girls sort of started to snarl and gather around, holding their sticks menacingly, ready to defend their coach.

Coach Norton, who had been at the other end of the field with Coach Jerra drilling the forwards, saw Laura gesturing wildly as she screamed and came toward us like a woman on a mission. "You are not supposed to be here," Coach Norton said as she pulled Laura off the field. Laura had third period gym with Coach Norton. Laura was screaming and crying as Coach Norton led her away.

"Who the hell was that?" Karen asked in dismay.

"Morgan's sister," Deanna said darkly. They had a few classes together.

Coach Anderson, still looking angry, blew the whistle announcing the end of practice. "Showers," she said, then added quickly "Except you, Morgan. Stay here please."

The other players sort of looked at each other, anticipating that something was going to happen— and didn't leave the field.

Coach Jerra exchanged a look with Coach Anderson, then shouted, "Okay ladies, let's go! Showers!" She clapped her hands together and the girls started off the pitch, albeit somewhat reluctantly.

I stood there, cringing and embarrassed and a little frightened as Coach Anderson walked up to me. She took a hold of the face mask of my helmet and jostled it gently as she asked, "Are you in there, Morgan? Do you want to talk about it?"

"My sister is nuts. My parents are fighting." I replied succinctly.

Coach Anderson chuckled as she let go of the mask and stepped back, looking at her feet as she continued, "That sums it up nicely. Are you okay?"

"Yes, ma'am!" I said, putting my stick on my left shoulder like a rifle as I braced at attention.

"Do you want to talk about it?"

"No, ma'am!"

"Are you sure?"

"Yes, ma'am!"

Coach Anderson sort of snorted, then came to attention herself as she announced, "You're gonna make a hell of a Marine, Flynn!" This was a compliment of the highest order from Coach Anderson.

I brought my right hand up in a salute. "Thank you, ma'am!"

Smiling slightly, Coach Anderson returned the salute and barked playfully, "Fall out, Flynn! Showers! Double time!"

I sprinted back to the locker room.

My day did not get any better. During social studies one of the kids who worked as an office assistant came in and handed the teacher a note. I was wanted in the principal's office. I was surprised as I had never been called to the office before. I had seen Principal Newton around campus — he always wore gray and didn't seem to notice anyone but the seniors.

The lady with the beehive hairdo at the front desk was waiting for me. "Is this about this morning?" I asked. She sort of shrugged at me and hit the intercom button to tell him I was there.

"Send her in," came the reply. I got the surprise of my life when I walked in and saw Mr. and Mrs. Mathews sitting on the couch. They both looked upset.

"What are you doing here?" I sputtered.

They both got to their feet and Mrs. Mathews cried "Where is Butchie?"

"I don't know!" I replied, confused. How would I know where he was?

Mr. and Mrs. Mathews started talking at once, telling me that I needed to come clean about the whereabouts of their son. Mr. Newton raised his voice and got them to calm down and sit down, then he addressed me. "We understand that you know where Butch Mathews is?"

"No, I don't." I shook my head.

"Morgan, this is not a game!" Mr. Mathews thundered. I saw where Suzy got her angry face from.

I flinched at the volume, and Mrs. Morgan grabbed her husband's arm saying, "Dennis...please..." Then she turned to me. "Morgan, think hard — do you have any idea where Butchie is?"

"No, ma'am, I don't. Who said I know where he is?"

Mr. Newton cleared his throat. "Your sister Laura was in here earlier today. She said that you know where Butch is."

"She's lying." I sputtered.

"I swear Morgan, if you are lying" — Mr. Mathews began, but was cut off when Mr. Newton asked "Morgan, when was the last time you talked to Butch?"

I thought for a moment. "Suzy's graduation party last spring." I looked at Mr. and Mrs. Mathews. "I don't even see him at school. We don't run with the same crowd."

"You're not part of his group?" Mrs. Mathews asked.

"Not at all. He's a Back Gater. I'm a jock," I replied, making Mr. Newton smirk.

"Why would your sister say you know where he is?" Mr. Mathews demanded.

"I don't know."

There was a pause, then Mr. Mathews muttered something about not having time for games and stood up, taking his wife's hand to leave. Mr. Newton got to his feet and opened the door, telling them he planned to talk to several students and said he would call if he heard anything.

I started to leave but Mr. Newton said, "Stay here, Morgan."

I stood there while he closed the door and returned to his seat. On his desk was a manila folder with my name on it.

"Do you know what this is, Morgan?" He turned it around so I could see it better. "This is your permanent record."

"Okay." I just looked at him, perplexed. "Why are you showing me this?"

He leveled his gaze at me. "Morgan, you are smart. Some might say 'scary smart.'"

I went cold and started to tremble. "I don't know what that means."

Before he could explain the intercom chime sounded. I jumped at the sound as the secretary's voice came through, announcing Coach Norton had arrived.

"I'm sorry, I was on the field and it took awhile to find me," she said as she entered. She drew up short when she saw me there. "Oh! Morgan! Good, you're here."

"Coach, what's going on?" I yelped.

Coach Norton locked eyes with Principal Newton, then she sort of took a breath. "Morgan, as if this morning at practice wasn't enough, Laura had a meltdown today after gym class. She said that you know where Butch Mathews is and… that you tried to kill your mother."

My knees went weak and I sank onto the couch.

"None of that's true!"

Coach Norton joined me on the couch, explaining that she had brought Laura to speak to the school counselor that morning. Laura told the counselor that our parents were fighting and might get divorced because of me. The counselor got Laura settled down, then sent her to class. Laura had third period gym and was chronically late to her fourth period class. After seven tardies it was automatic detention. Laura argued that she shouldn't get detention because the tardy wasn't her fault as she didn't have enough time to shower and dress and do her hair because of the length of gym class. The teacher gave Laura a detention slip anyway, and Laura went ballistic and was promptly sent to the office. She screamed at Mr. Newton that they should really be focusing their attention on her psycho dyke sister who "tried to kill her mother and is hiding Butch Mathews" then she stormed out. There was a meeting between Mr. Newton and the school counselor, then they called the Mathews', figuring being called to the principal's office and facing them would break me, and I would tell them where Butch was.

My voice rose in frustration as I said, "I already told you, I don't know where Butch Mathews is! What does this have to do with my permanent record?"

Mr. Newton said, "I thought it prudent to look at your record to see if there are behavior problems there."

"Did you find any?" I asked, my voice cracking.

"No," He paused, then began slowly, "However, you have a very high IQ and sometimes people with high IQs do terrible things just because they can."

"I am not following at all!" I was in tears I was so frustrated. *High IQ my butt*, I thought.

Coach Norton cleared her throat. "He means... sometimes people with high IQs can be manipulative — as in making people jump through hoops, doing mean things, just for entertainment."

"That's not me," I shook my head. "If I ever want to do mean things, I do them on paper."

Mr. Newton smiled. "Ah yes — your record says you have quite the writing talent. What kind of stories do you write, Morgan?"

"Mostly stories about kids who want to get away from their families," I said with a shrug. "I write what I know. Lots of my characters are runaways."

"Have you written stories about killing your mother? According to Laura you hate your mother so much you tried to kill her or want to kill her. Did you write something like that, Morgan?" he pressed.

"No!" I roared. "I don't write that kind of stuff! I've never let Laura read any of my stories — " Then it hit me. "I think she's talking about when I was born?" I stammered. "I was eight weeks premature. There were complications and Laura says Mom almost died."

Coach Norton let out a gasp. "Oh, good God," she muttered.

"You couldn't control your birth," Then she addressed Mr. Newton, saying, "Laura Flynn is rather high-strung."

I didn't know what that meant, but Mr. Newton sort of rolled his eyes and nodded his head like he did.

Coach Anderson was waiting for me when I got to afternoon practice. She said we had to adjust the helmet to fit me better, because she noticed it looked a little loose that morning. She had me in the office for about fifteen minutes as she adjusted the chin strap. She was really delaying me so that Coach Norton could tell the girls NOT to mention the scene with Laura from that morning. Her exact words, according to Deanna, were, "Morgan doesn't need that."

As I walked onto the field, the rest of the team was warming up. Winnifred was on the slope taking her flute out of the case. She was glancing around as if looking for someone or something.

"Play some Beatles!" Coach Anderson shouted and Winnifred obligingly launched into, *You've Got to Hide Your Love Away*.

I think the helmet gave me extra confidence because I was so aggressive during drills that after a few minutes Coach Norton put me in the goal against the varsity players and Coach Anderson cautioned me to dial it back.

Suzy was late to practice. I overheard her apologizing to Coach Norton -- she said she'd been driving around looking for her brother. I wasn't sure if she was angry at me like her parents were, so I did my best to avoid her. I don't think she noticed though, she seemed awfully distracted.

At 4:20 p.m., Coach Norton called it quits. Suzy was one of the first to leave the field. I didn't want to go home yet, so I asked if anyone would like to stay a bit later to take shots on the goal so that I could get used to the helmet. Coach Jerra, Deanna and two other forwards from the JV obliged, and I was able to stretch out my day for another twenty minutes until Coach Jerra called time and told us to hit the showers.

Part of the reason I wanted to stretch out the day was that I didn't want to run into Suzy on the way home. I might if she was driving around the neighborhood looking for her brother, so I took the creek path. The path started in a ravine behind the high school and meandered next to the creek until it dumped out in the park about a block from my house. My plan worked beautifully until I rounded the curve by the grove of trees next to the parking lot and there was Suzy's car a mere seventy feet away and Suzy, still in her coach's uniform, was sitting on the hood with her head down and her arms folded on her chest. She had her back to me. Winnifred was next to her. I froze. Winnifred had her hand on Suzy's shoulder and was saying something. I was too far away to hear. Suzy got to her feet and turned to face Winnifred, her face crumpled in tears. Winnifred pulled Suzy in for a hug. Suzy permitted this, then Winnifred stepped back and tilted Suzy's face up and kissed her on the lips, then embraced her and kissed the top of her head. So that was why Winnifred watched the games and now the practices! She was watching Suzy. It was an unmistakably intimate, private moment of tenderness, and I felt dirty for witnessing it.

There was no way I could get to the street without walking past them, so I started to back up, intending to hike all the way back to school because I didn't want to disturb them, but I wasn't fast enough. Winnifred looked up and locked eyes with me. The color drained from her face, and I read her lips as she said, "There's Morgan,"

Suzy whipped her head around and looked at me. She looked surprised and horrified and she blushed bright red as she jumped away from Winnifred like she was on fire.

We stared at each other like wolves in a Jack London novel. "Morgan!" Suzy cried as she took a hesitant step toward me.

I shook my head and turned and ran away as fast as I could go. I don't know why I ran, it just seemed like the right thing to do. I was sprinting, which was hard to do since I was wearing a backpack loaded with books. I realized that if Suzy gave chase, she could probably catch me because she was faster, so I jumped off the path and dove into the underbrush to hide. The plants were wet because of the rain, so I got soaked as I hunkered down in vegetation. I was glad my backpack was olive drab and allowed me to blend into the brush.

My junior commando techniques worked. Suzy ran past me, calling my name, then after a few minutes she came back, red-faced out of breath. I watched as she sort of looked around for a moment, then lifted her arms and let them fall at her sides in a gesture of resignation, then jogged back to the parking lot.

I started shaking all over. I wasn't sure if it was cold or something else. I curled up small as it started to rain. I just stayed there, shivering and starting to cry and becoming part of the forest.

CHAPTER 9

We Need to Talk

$\mathcal{I}$t was nearly dark by the time I extricated myself from the brush and headed home. I was soaking wet and cold. I felt hurt and confused and wasn't sure why.

I was a full two hours late. My parents were greatly relieved when I walked in the door. It had been a tough day for them. The school had called about Laura's meltdown. Mrs. Mathews called to apologize for scaring me and Suzy had called looking for me.

Mom sat me down at the kitchen table and grilled me. Where the hell had I been? Did I know how worried they were? Why was I shivering? Was I on something?

Dad grabbed the candy-striped LL Bean trapper blanket from the end of my bed and wrapped it around my shoulders while I answered Mom's questions. I was late because I had to walk home because Laura had flattened the tires on my bike (again) and practice had gone long, and I was moving slowly because the coach had worked us really hard, and I was sore. I was shivering because it was raining and I was soaked because the two cotton sweatshirts and windbreaker I wore didn't do much to keep me warm or dry.

"I told you that if you lost weight I would get you a winter coat," Mom scowled. "I don't know why you won't do that!"

"Jennifer! This is your child!" Dad scolded, putting his hands on my shoulders. He added softly, almost apologetically, "My child too."

Mom started to cry and apologized for trashing my room the night before, but said I made her do it, so technically it was my fault. I didn't agree with that at all but knew better than to argue. Laura was grounded and made to stay in her room with no telephone or television, and on the advice of the school counselor my folks were taking her to a child psychologist. They asked if I wanted to see one too. I said no, then asked about going to boarding school. I said the family would likely be a lot happier if I went away — Laura had been saying this for years. That made Mom cry more. Dad just looked sad, but like he knew where I was coming from.

Dad offered to make me one of his famous scrambled egg concoctions for dinner, but I demurred, saying I had a stomach ache and asked to be excused to my room. Dad sort of smiled as he walked me up the stairs, then he reached into the pocket of his shirt and retrieved a Hershey bar. He handed it to me with a nod — it was an apology. Dad loved chocolate and so did I. It was our secret thing.

I took a shower then put on the sweats I wore as pajamas. I was sitting on my bed trying to do my homework when I was startled by a tapping on the window. I pushed back the curtains and there was Suzy on the roof, soaking wet, still in her coach's uniform. She had climbed the oak tree next to the house to get access to the roof. I had done it a few times myself.

I opened the window. "What are you doing here? Why didn't you use the front door?"

"I didn't want to deal with your family," she said through chattering teeth.

"That makes two of us," I said, putting my hands on my hips. "Where do your parents think you are?"

"Out looking for Butchie." She looked at me, her eyes welling with tears. "We need to talk."

As Suzy somewhat clumsily entered my room I jammed my desk chair under the doorknob so no one could open the door from the outside. I grabbed the blanket I'd been wearing earlier and handed it to her.

"Thank you," she sniffed as she put it around herself. She wasn't wearing any shoes, and her socks were wet and muddy.

"Where the hell are your shoes?" I demanded.

"Have you ever tried to climb a tree wearing soccer cleats?" she cried indignantly.

I gestured for her to sit on the bed close to the heater vent on the floor. I sat at the head of the bed, as far away from her as I could get, waiting for her to speak.

Suzy sort of held the blanket open to bring the warm air in, then began timidly, "I would appreciate it if you didn't tell anyone about today."

"What part of today?" I asked acidly. "The part where my sister went nuts in front of the team? The part where your parents accused me of being a liar and knowing where your brother is? The part where my sister told Mr. Newton and the school counselor I tried to kill Mom and I know where Butch is, the part where Mr. Newton described me as some sort of evil genius, or the part when I walked up on you and Winnifred making out in the parking lot?"

Suzy's head snapped up and her eyes were hard. "Don't you dare call it that! Don't you dare make it dirty!" she hissed. Her lower lip trembled as tears of anger slid down her face.

"Whoa!" I recoiled, surprised by her reaction. "I'm sorry, I didn't mean to come off so harsh!"

"Oh sure, like you didn't mean to be harsh when you said what you said about Rick!" Suzy spat.

"Wow," my throat swelled, and I started to tremble. I got off the bed and backed away like she was holding a weapon on me. "I thought you had forgiven me for that. I'm sorry! I don't why I said something so awful,"

"I think it's because you like to go for the jugular," Suzy glared at me. "You are really, really sensitive, and you use that biting wit like a weapon. Hurt the other person before they can hurt you!"

My eyes filled with tears. "Ouch!" I looked away, trying to hold back the sobs. I didn't like the idea of being sensitive, because to me it was the same as being weak.

"You are angry all the time," Suzy said, her voice rising. "I see it. Other people see it. Instead of lashing out and hurting other people, maybe you should figure out what you're so angry about?"

"Right back at you," I said, turning to face her. "You can be pretty nasty when you want to be!"

Suzy's voice cracked as she replied, "I know."

There was a pause as we both tried to get control of ourselves. After a moment, I blurted out "You love Winnifred, don't you?"

Suzy blushed and dropped her eyes. "I do, very much," Then she looked up at me, tearful and vulnerable as she warbled, "Please don't tell anyone what you saw."

"I won't," my voice cracked. "I apologize for intruding. It was obviously a very tender moment. It looked like she was comforting you. You obviously care for each other deeply."

"We do," Suzy nodded. "She's very special to me and I want to protect her." She wiped tears from her face as she said, "Please don't tell anyone. Please don't hurt her."

"I won't!" I held up my left hand and crossed my heart with my right hand. "Scout's Honor! I swear on my hockey stick and the soul of Coach Norton that I won't tell!"

"Thank you," Suzy chuckled at my choice of reverence.

"How long have you and Winnifred been... together?" I wasn't sure what the correct terminology was.

"Three years," Suzy smiled.

"Wow," I blinked. Three years was an eternity in high school.

"She was my first kiss that meant anything," Suzy sighed wistfully.

"Did you get bats in your stomach?" I asked.

"Do you mean butterflies?" Suzy asked, giving me a funny look.

"No, bats. I got bats the first time I kissed Kevin," I shrugged. I wasn't sure if it was because I really liked him, because it was my first kiss, or because I was worried his braces would get in the way.

"No, no bats, but an incredible feeling of joy and warmth and tenderness," Suzy sighed, her eyes shining at the memory.

"Wow," I was impressed. "How long have you known that you were...you know?"

"Gay? The word is gay," Suzy said, amused at my discomfort. "The fourth grade."

"The fourth grade? Are you serious?" I stared at her.

"Yes, I got a crush on the girl that sat next to me. She had a Mickey Mouse book bag." Suzy smirked sheepishly. "Something about it just did it for me I guess."

"Oh, I totally get it," I nodded. "A Mickey Mouse book bag might turn my head too." That made Suzy laugh and cry at the same time.

"I'm so sorry my parents jumped all over you," she sniffed. "I told them you didn't know anything about Butch and it was just Laura being ugly. My parents think he ran away." Suzy continued. "He took his bike and his backpack with him."

"That's better than him being kidnapped," I said. Kids at school had been talking about that.

"I'm hoping for runway," Suzy agreed as she sort of leaned over and hugged herself. She took a deep breath and burst out with, "It's been a really crappy day, Morgan! Butchie disappears, then Winnifred tells me she is moving back to Scotland in a month. It's been a really rotten day!" Then she buried her face in her hands and started to bawl hysterically. Her whole body shook as she cried so hard tears squeezed through her fingers.

I didn't know what to say so I sat down next to her and put my arms around her and let her cry. She buried her face in my shoulder and sobbed. I had never held her in my arms like this – I had never comforted anyone like this before. I felt strong and protective and as though our roles had reversed.

Between sobs Suzy explained that Winnifred's parents were divorced and had shared custody. Winnifred had to go back to Scotland because she had dual citizenship. She would finish high school there, then return to the states for college.

"Do your folks know about you two?" I asked gently.

Suzy looked at me like I was crazy. "Oh, good God, no! They're too wrapped up in Butchie's behavior. As long as my grades are good and I don't come home pregnant, I'm off their radar,"

"I'm in the same boat," I sighed.

"You are?" Suzy asked, wiping her face with her sleeve.

"Yes. Laura is bat-crap crazy and Mom and Dad are always cleaning up after her. That boat you are in? I'm first oarsman!"

That made Suzy chuckle. She added that she was sure that Winnifred's parents didn't know about their relationship because if they did, the shit would have hit the fan a long time ago.

"We think her mom almost figured it out a few years ago. She was worried we spent too much time together. Fred played field hockey one season. She was on the JV with me."

"Fred?"

"My pet name for her."

"Ah-ha! And what does she call you?" I smiled.

Suzy blushed shyly. "She calls me Suze," she dropped her eyes, adding, "No one else calls me that."

"As it should be," I nodded, squeezing her shoulder.

A knock at the door made us both jump. "Morgan? Are you decent?" It was Dad. He always knocked.

Suzy let out a gasp. I slapped my hand over her mouth and whispered, "Get behind the bed." Suzy, my hand still over her mouth, nodded quickly. She handed me the blanket then went behind the bed.

I waited a few seconds for Suzy to get out of sight, then tossed the blanket on the bed and moved the chair so I could open the door. Dad was standing in the hallway holding a green metal steamer trunk like the ones kids take to college. It had a hasp and a key, and he also had a new padlock in his hand.

"What's up Dad?" I asked.

"Did I hear you talking to someone?" Dad asked suspiciously.

I felt a stab of fear, but I replied "Trying out dialog, Dad. For a story?"

"Oh...okay." He seemed to accept that, and he opened the door wider so he could put the trunk in my room. "This is for you. If your mother won't allow a lock on the door at least you can put whatever in this trunk and lock it away." He handed me the padlock. "Here you go."

"Thanks, Dad!" I was surprised. I knew I'd be putting lots of stories in it.

"Open it."

I did. Inside the trunk was Dad's M65 field jacket from the Marines. It still had his name tape on it. I looked at him in surprise. Dad kept his old uniforms in his footlocker in the attic. Laura and I were under strict orders not to touch them.

Dad sort of shrugged. "It's yours to wear. It's about three sizes too big for you, but it's warm."

"Thanks Dad!" I put it on. It nearly reached my knees.

He nodded, then looked at me, so sad, as he said, "Please don't run away, Morgan. Your mother and I have problems, but please don't think you're the reason we're fighting. We have our own issues."

I got a lump in my throat. "Dad..." I began. "Please send me away! I don't want to be here anymore! I love you, but Mom and Laura are killing me. It's pretty rotten when you don't feel safe or welcome in your own home."

"I know," Dad said softly as he hugged me, holding me for what seemed like a long time. "Just keep busy and out of their way,"

"Easier said than done, Dad," I spat, then I told him how Laura had crashed field hockey practice and called Coach Anderson a dyke.

Dad looked pained. "Should I call Coach Anderson and explain to her? Maybe apologize to her?"

"No, Dad, she's tough, she's a Marine." I replied, as Dad had taught me there was no such thing as an ex-Marine.

"Okay," Dad nodded with approval and then ruffled my hair playfully as he said, "don't stay up too late studying."

"I won't," my voice was thick with emotion.

I closed the door then put the chair and trunk in front of it just in case Dad tried to come back in. I wiped away the tears then whispered, "It's okay, Suzy, you can come out now, but keep your voice down."

When Suzy came out from under the bed her face was red and she was crying. "Morgan, I am so sorry! I had no idea you were so unhappy."

"Please don't tell anyone," I pleaded, my voice shaking.

"I won't," she wiped her face on her sleeve and forced a smile as she said, "You are a cool liar. I bet that's what Mr. Newton meant by evil genius!"

"I know," I said, handing Suzy the blanket again. She wrapped it around herself and we returned to our places on the side of the bed.

Suzy looked at me. "Nice jacket."

"Thanks."

We were quiet for a moment, then Suzy asked, "Did Laura really call Coach Anderson a dyke?"

"Yes, and accused her of being my lesbian lover,"

Suzy shook her head. "Coach Anderson isn't gay,"

"That's right she's married," I nodded.

Suzy made a face. "Oh, that doesn't have anything to do with it. I know she's not gay because the time I kissed her she didn't open her mouth."

I guess the look on my face was priceless because Suzy's eyes bugged out and she slapped both hands over her mouth to cover the sound of her laughing. She actually slid off the bed shaking in hysterics. I watched her rolling around like a landed salmon, then went over to my desk and started writing.

"What are you writing?" Suzy gasped when she had recovered her composure.

"I'm writing that one down," I said. "That was funny!"

Suzy grinned then returned to warming herself over the heater. There was a moment of silence, then Suzy burst out with, "So what is happening with you and Kevin? Are you still together?"

"I don't know," I shrugged, thinking it an odd segue. Truth be told I rarely saw Kevin once school started. We saw each other at morning break, but during lunch he hung out in the math lab playing Dungeons and Dragons with a bunch of other boys. I had no interest in that.

Suzy gave me a funny look.

"You don't know? Shouldn't that be the kind of thing you know?"

I sighed. "We only see each other at school. He wants to have sex. He says if I don't do it with him it means that I don't love him."

Suzy rolled her eyes. "Oh, that is such bullshit! Guys always say that! How old is he?"

"Fourteen, like me."

Suzy let out a snort. "Fourteen is too young to be having sex! You're too young! You're too irresponsible! You're too immature!" she said, sounding like the strong, opinionated Suzy I knew and was more comfortable with.

"I'm not arguing," I shrugged. "He says if I don't do it, it will mean I'm gay."

Suzy's face twisted in scorn. "That's not what it means! Not wanting to have sex when you're fourteen doesn't mean you're gay!" She looked me up and down. "Does your plumbing work? Are you using any birth control?"

I blushed. "Oh, good God, are we really having this conversation?" I moaned, cringing. "Yes, the plumbing works! No, we haven't done anything to test it."

That made her relax a little.

"Any guy who gives you the 'you would if you loved me' line isn't worth it. You're not ready — he's probably not ready either but he's too stupid to know it," she scowled.

We sat for a few minutes in silence, then I said, "I kind of figured I'd be one of those girls who was drunk on her wedding night and saved it for her husband?"

"There is nothing wrong with that," Suzy said evenly, looking relieved.

CHAPTER 10

The Death of Coach Norton

I graduated the day after my 18th birthday and went to college at North State University, the northern-most campus in the California State University system. It was the farthest I could get from home without paying out of state tuition. I was anxious to leave home, mostly to get away from Laura, so much so that I tried to take the GED and join the Air Force at the age of seventeen, but I needed both parents to sign off because I was still a minor and Mom refused. She said I would never get a husband if I joined the military.

Laura graduated from high school and lived at home while she took classes at the community college. She got a part-time job at Sears where she met Kyle who became her boyfriend and later husband and father of her children. She resented me for graduating a semester early and attending a four-year institution, although she was happy when I left.

I was studying journalism. My college experience was typical until October of my junior year when Mom died suddenly of a heart attack. It was unexpected and jarring — especially for Laura, who was recently married and pregnant. I missed several weeks of school because I came home to help Dad with things. Laura was next to useless, so it was up to me to help Dad with the arrangements. I felt more numb than anything else — but I had to be a good soldier for Dad, so I made lists of tasks to accomplish. Dad was big on checklists because of his experience as an aerospace engineer and had instilled their use in me.

In December, Dad went to an office Christmas party with a woman he worked with. Laura said it was too soon and a betrayal of Mom's memory. Dad argued they were just friends, but Laura got so angry that when she and Kyle moved into a new apartment she didn't give Dad her new telephone number or address. She still had her key to the house though. When Dad was at work she came over and helped herself to home furnishings, food, you name it. Dad told her to stop -- and demanded she hand over her key. She refused and told Dad if he tried to keep her out of the house he would never see his grandchild. But Dad had enough of her — he responded by changing the locks and then the telephone number because she kept crank calling him.

In January, Dad called to tell me that Coach Norton had died from a heart attack. She was just a year away from retirement. There was a memorial service planned at the high school in late February. It coincided with college winter break, and since Coach Norton had been such a big influence on me, I went home for the event — and was surprised to learn I would be on my own that week because Dad was on a business trip.

It felt weird to be in the house by myself, although I welcomed the quiet. Too much had happened too quickly, and I mean more than the family drama. When Mom died the first thing I thought was "I can be gay now" and like an answer to that, I suddenly developed a crush on the woman who played sweeper for the newly created NSU field hockey club. Her name was Nikki, but everyone called her Gator because she was from Florida and always wore a Lacoste jacket. She was a big blonde girl, very gay and very out. We were both journalism majors and had several classes together and worked at KNSU, the school radio station. She was a production engineer and I was learning to be one. We had back-to-back radio shows. She had a doo-wop and Motown show on Friday night and I followed with a British Invasion show. Toward the end of the semester, I foolishly told her that I had feelings for her as the Beatles *Til There Was You* was playing. She laughed, telling me she was flattered, but not interested, because I was too young for her -- I was four years her junior and in her words, 'too much of a jock'. After that, whenever she saw me she would tease me by asking if I still had feelings for her. Embarrassed, I avoided her as much as I could — I was glad to be gone from school for a week because playing Avoid the Dyke was exhausting.

Coach Norton's memorial service was held on Saturday in the high school cafeteria. The room was decorated with black and gold streamers and the tables and walls were covered with pho-tographs of Coach Norton and the teams she had shepherded over decades. There were over a hundred people crowded into the cafeteria, many of them wearing their letterman jackets and team jerseys. There was a short video about Coach Norton's life, then a few of her former students and coworkers spoke, then Coach Norton's sister, who was presiding over the event, made sure everyone had a glass of champagne and we drank a toast. I took a glass although I was underage. After the toast we were invited to mingle and look at all the photographs on display.

I was looking at a photograph of the track team my freshmen year when I heard a familiar voice behind me say, "Nice jacket!"

I turned around to see Suzy Mathews smiling at me. She was dressed in black slacks and a black and silver silk blouse. Her hair was way shorter than I had seen it before and she had a partially empty champagne glass in her hand. She was wearing her letterman jacket which was covered with much more athletic and academic bling than mine because in addition to playing multiple sports she had been on the student council and in the honor society.

"Hello Suzy," I grinned.

Her smile broadened. "Morgan Flynn! How long has it been?"

"Oh! At least three years?" I had to think. We'd lost contact when she went away to college.

She gave me a look and pointed to the glass in my hand. "Are you old enough to be drinking that?"

"No comment."

Suzy let out a bark of laughter. "Come here, give me a hug!" she cried, throwing her arm around me. I was surprised at how skinny she was.

"What are you up to these days?" she asked when we separated.

"Going to college. Studying journalism. Learning to fly for a career in the Air Force just in case journalism doesn't work out."

Suzy's eyes went wide. "You're a pilot in the Air Force?"

"I might be," I said.

I told her how I planned to attend Officer's Candidate School after I completed my degree. Although women weren't allowed to fly combat, I wanted to fly a cargo aircraft. I figured if I could find a way to combine flying and writing I would have it made.

"You look very fit," Suzy said, sweeping her eyes up and down me again.

"So do you. What have you been up to?" I asked.

"I'm a vegetarian — that takes the pounds off – and I'm a marine biologist," She explained that despite her parent's protests she had transferred to a four-year university and emerged with a bachelor's degree in biology. She was working at a small animal rehab facility on the coast while slowly working on her master's degree, because that would put her in the running for a job at the San Francisco aquarium. She was telling me about donning a wetsuit to get in the tide pool tank with the orphaned baby sea otters when Joan, one of our field hockey teammates appeared. Joan was over six feet tall and had red hair pulled back in a monstrous ponytail. Joan was three years ahead of me in school and a year behind Suzy.

"I see female hockey players!" Joan announced as she approached us. "Hello Spunky! Hello Traffic Ticket!"

"Traffic Ticket?" I repeated, looking at Suzy.

"That's what we called this one," Joan beamed, throwing

her arm around Suzy. "Our esteemed former teammate turned assistant coach! A third of the team had crushes on her because she had fine written all over her — hence Traffic Ticket!"

Suzy's eyes went wide. "What? Are you sure it was me?" she squeaked, blushing.

"Oh yes," Joan grinned like a wicked colt then glanced around surreptitiously then pulled a silver flask out of her suit jacket and offered it to Suzy. "Whiskey – just like on that road trip!" she grinned.

Suzy's eyes gleamed and she took the flask, took a slug, then handed it to me. I took a snort and handed it back to Joan. I had no idea what road trip Joan was talking about, but I wanted to be one of the girls.

"There's a bunch of us meeting on the tennis courts to drink a toast to Coach Norton," Joan said in a low voice.

Suzy nodded then looked at me. "I'm game! You game, Morgan?"

"Sure," I nodded and we followed Joan out the back door.

As we walked across campus Suzy leaned into me to explain, "At memorials like this it is very important to form a sub party,"

"Yes, ma'am. Of course, ma'am," I nodded. The whiskey was hitting me already.

Sub party was right! In the shelter next to the tennis court someone had set up a pony keg and decades of high school athletes were drinking from red plastic party cups. Pretty soon there were over fifty of us reminiscing and drinking toasts to our former coach. We made it a rule that every time someone said "coach" you had to drink. It wasn't long before we were all drunk and singing the school fight song. The party broke up when the police arrived, two cops actually, because someone who lived near the school had complained about the noise. One of the cops was a Wilson High graduate — he had been on the student council with Suzy. He told us as long as no one attempted to drive, we could go on our way.

Suzy, drunk, asked me to walk her home saying she wasn't sure she remembered the way. Also drunk I braced at attention as I barked, "Allow me to escort you home, ma'am!"

Suzy gave me a sloppy salute. "Thank you, soldier."

I held out my elbow. She took my arm and we somewhat drunkenly marched — or rather I marched and she staggered — the three blocks to her house.

Suzy talked a blue streak on the way home, telling me how much she wanted the job in San Francisco and how her parents were not happy with her career choice. "I'm almost twenty-six. I think they just want me to get married and pregnant," she said as she fumbled with her keys at the front door. She pushed open the door and pulled me inside. We fell over each other, landing on the floor in the entryway.

"Mom! Dad! I'm home!" Suzy shouted, getting unsteadily to her feet and dragging me with her. "And I'm drunk! And I brought a friend! She's drunk too!"

"Shhh! Are you crazy?" I admonished.

Suzy gave me a wicked smile and grabbed me by the front of my jacket and started pulling me deeper into the house. "They're not home and they're not going to be home until Tuesday. I was going to be in town for the memorial anyway, so I am house sitting for them."

"What about Butch?" I asked warily.

Suzy made a dismissive noise. "He's doing time in Colorado for a DUI," and she put her finger to her lips as she added, "But don't tell anyone that — my parents tell people he's in the Peace Corps."

"Noted," I said, taken aback. I had never seen Suzy like this before and it made me uneasy.

Suzy giggled as she pulled me into the hallway that was filled with family photographs — but none of Rick. And as if that wasn't weird enough, the ones with Suzy and Butch in them appeared to end with their early high school years. The three most prominent pictures were her parent's wedding day and Suzy's high school and college graduation photos.

"They had to put up both of my graduation pictures because Butch didn't graduate," Suzy snorted, "Thus cementing my role as the golden child," she chanted in a sing-song voice. "It all falls to me! My big brother is gone, my little brother is a waste case! I am the only one left!"

"Heavy," I said, wondering how her parents would react to seeing the golden child drunk.

"Our tour continues!" Suzy cried as she pulled me upstairs. "Here we go, the highlight of our tour," she pushed open the door to her childhood bedroom as she shouted dramatically, "Behold! The place where time stopped!"

She wasn't kidding. The walls were still avocado green, the walk-in closet still had a Rolling Stones poster on the door, the full-length mirror was on the wall, there was the same full-sized bed with the rainbow comforter and all those sports trophies were still stacked on the bookcase.

"Oh, that's just weird," I remarked, surveying her room. "Nothing has changed!"

"That's my parents doing, they kept it as a shrine," she shook her head ruefully. "I've been out of the house for six years and they still think I am coming home."

I caught sight of myself in the full-length mirror. "I can't believe I worked so hard for this stupid jacket!" I sighed.

My high school goals had been lettering in sports, and getting a good score on the Scholastic Aptitude Test thinking the combination would get me into a good college. Mom said I was lazy, therefore I would need a scholarship, tons of extracurricular activities, and possibly divine intervention to get into a decent school. I said as much to Suzy.

"That's bullshit," Suzy snorted, joining me in front of the mirror. "Look at this! So many extracurricular activities!" she said, gesturing to her jacket. "And for what? A two-year field hockey scholarship to the community college! Practice six days a week and go to school full-time! Transfer to a four-year and repeat! Being the last hope of the Mathews family nearly killed me!"

"We look like Wilson High threw up," I sighed as we stood side by side, looking at ourselves sporting the black and gold jackets with the chenille letters and the patches and pins for the accomplishments and activities that had dominated our teen years.

Suzy's eyes widened. "Remember the year the field hockey team had that assistant coach who had been on the U.S. Olympic team? So much barfing!"

I frowned. "I don't remember that. I think it was before my time. Do you remember when we got Coach Norton mad at us and almost had to go home in those gym towels?"

Suzy shuddered. "Oh yes!"

"I was scared to death!"

Suzy chuckled. "More like you were embarrassed. You apologized. I apologized. I was contrite. You were contrite. We both learned our lesson."

Her eyes met mine in the mirror. She put her arm around my waist and pulled me closer as she whispered in my ear, "and you sure grew up good."

Her words surprised me, and I turned to look at her and the next thing I knew I was kissing her right on the lips. It felt warm and tender and oh, so right.

"Oh my," I gasped when we parted, surprised at what had just happened, at what I had just done. "That was —"

"Wonderful," Suzy sighed and we sank down onto the bed.

A few hours later the sound of a door slamming made me bolt awake. I looked at Suzy, who was also awake, looking as surprised as I was. We were both naked under the covers.

"Is this a dream?" I gasped as we heard someone moving around downstairs.

"More like a nightmare! Get dressed!" Suzy said frantically, struggling to sit up in bed. "Damn it, I'm still drunk!"

She wasn't the only one. My head was pounding, and the bed was spinning.

"Suzy? Are you up there?" It was Mr. Mathews.

"Oh shit! Hurry up!" Suzy admonished, lunging out of bed to grab my clothes from the floor. She threw them at me. "Get your clothes on! Get in the closet!"

"So on the nose," I muttered, pulling my underwear on under the covers. "I thought you said your parents were gone for the weekend?"

"They're supposed to be!" Suzy gasped, just as the door to her room opened and Mr. Mathews stepped into the room.

"We got about a fourth of the way to the cabin when the check engine light came on in the car and your mother —" Mr. Mathews was saying. He broke off and his eyes hardened when he saw us.

Suzy dove for the bed, covering herself with the sheet as she squeaked indignantly "Daddy! You're supposed to knock!" The red was climbing in her face. "What are you doing home? I thought you and Mom were going to be gone until Tuesday?"

Mr. Mathews opened his mouth to reply as Mrs. Mathews walked in. "Is Suzy up here?" she asked. She took one look at us and let out a shriek followed by "Oh my Lord!"

"No, Morgan Flynn," I offered up, modestly clutching the comforter. I couldn't resist trying to add some levity to the situation, but it fell flat as all three of the Mathews clan glared at me.

"Oh God, shut up Morgan," Suzy moaned, wincing as if in pain.

Mr. Mathews stepped further into the room. He looked threatening and I immediately looked around for potential weapons. My eyes landed on a basketball trophy on the bookshelf. It was the largest one and I figured I could use it as a club if I had to.

"Suzanne Marie Mathews! I am so disappointed in you," Mr. Mathews snarled from the foot of the bed. "How dare you do this in our house!" he gestured to Mrs. Mathews who was standing in the doorway looking horrified and shaking her head.

"This is wrong!" Mrs. Mathews wailed, bursting into tears. "I failed! I failed!" She hurried out of the room, and we heard a door slam down the hall.

Mr. Mathews glared at me. "Was this your idea?"

Boy, did I blink! "Excuse me?"

"Dad, you and Mom weren't supposed to be home this weekend," Suzy's voice was plaintive. She glanced at me as she said, "Give us a moment to get it together and we can talk about this downstairs."

"There is nothing to talk about." Mr. Mathews spat. "You disgust me."

He turned on his heel and stomped away. There was a second door slam.

Suzy lunged out of bed, swearing blue and green as she grabbed her clothes off the floor and started to dress. "Get your clothes on! You have to leave!"

"With pleasure," I said breathlessly.

Suzy tossed me a look as she pulled on her blouse. "I'll try to calm them down," she said, rushing out the door.

Oh good luck with that, I thought. Down the hall I could hear Suzy in her parents' room — they were yelling and she was yelling, but I don't think they were hearing each other.

I scrambled into my clothes and quickly grabbed what I thought was my jacket from off the floor and ran for the stairs. Fight or flight, with the emphasis on the latter, was in play. I had made it to the front hall when Mr. Mathews bellowed my name and told me to stop. I turned around slowly, half afraid he had a gun. Fortunately, he didn't. He was on the stairs, Suzy was behind him looking scared.

"Morgan! How old are you?" Mr. Mathews demanded.

"What?" I was puzzled.

"How old are you?" he yelled again. He was shaking with rage. His eyes fell on the letterman jacket rolled up under my arm.

Behind him Suzy was shaking her head. It dawned on me what he was asking — he thought I was still in high school.

"Twenty," I said, turning to meet his gaze full-on. "I went to Coach Norton's memorial service at the school today. The high school letterman jacket was appropriate attire."

Mr. Mathews proceeded to call me every ugly thing he could think of or make up, there was a reference to jailbait, and he told me never to come near his daughter again. A number of snappy comebacks came to me, but Suzy was standing behind him looking terrified and shaking her head, warning me not to say anything. There was a horrible moment of silence, then I did a military style about-face and marched out, slamming the door behind me.

I hurried home, fighting tears all the way. Every time I heard a car coming from behind me I looked over my shoulder fearing it was Mr. Mathews. My head was pounding, and I was filled with regret. If only I hadn't gone to the memorial service – I never would have seen Suzy. This wouldn't have happened. I wondered how she managed to hide that aspect of her life from her parents all these years? In high school she had set off my dykedar — although I didn't know that's what it was called in those days. There was just something about her, a sort of energy. Some of the older girls referred to her as a "lipstick lesbian", a phrase I did not understand -- and there was that time her bra strap failed during field hockey practice. She was wearing a tank top and when the pink bra strap came flying out during a tackle several of the older girls got so distracted they ran into each other. Joan was one of them. Traffic Ticket, indeed.

I had been carrying the jacket rolled up under my arm like a football. When I got to my front door and reached into the pocket for my house keys, I discovered I had grabbed Suzy's jacket by mistake. It was adding insult to injury. I went around to the side of the house and used the oak tree outside my bedroom window to get access to the roof. I was lucky and the window was unlocked.

I tumbled in the window and threw the jacket across the room. This was a nightmare. It was more than having my courage come out of a bottle and outing Suzy to her parents. Losing my jacket, my house keys and Suzy in one afternoon seemed symbolic somehow. The jacket still meant a lot to me and Suzy meant a lot to me, and I was doubtful if I would ever see either one of them again. Especially Suzy. I had messed her life up and I was sure there was no going back.

A shower and aspirin had helped clear the hangover and a few hours later I was in sweats and sitting at my desk trying to write

Suzy a note of apology. The waste paper basket was overflowing with rejected attempts written on binder paper. *"Dear Suzy, I am soooooooooo sorry!"* I wrote for the umpteenth time when a tapping on the window startled me. I froze, wondering if it was my imagination, then the tapping came again.

I pushed back the curtains to see Suzy crouched on the roof in the dark. She was wearing jeans, sneakers, a UC Santa Cruz T-shirt and my jacket. She had a backpack slung over one shoulder. She looked upset.

I opened the window. "Hello, Suzy," I said tiredly. "You could have used the front door."

"I went with my strengths," she said. "I saw your light on. I have your jacket," she reached into the pocket. "And your keys," She held them out to me.

"Thanks," I took the keys. "I've got your jacket,"

Suzy nodded, then tearfully asked "Can I stay here tonight? My parents threw me out."

Before I could answer she started to sob. She cried so hard she lost her balance and I lunged through the window to grab her before she tumbled off the roof.

"Hey!" I cried, alarmed. "Get in here before you hurt yourself!" I half-dragged her inside. Both Suzy and her overstuffed backpack tumbled to the floor. The backpack spilled, and a quantity of tube socks, t-shirts, and a pink bra landed on the carpet. Obviously, she'd packed in a hurry.

"You brought the pink bra, I see," I tried to inject some levity into the situation.

"I never go anywhere without one," Suzy replied.

"I'm sorry I outed you to your parents," my tears matched hers.

"It wasn't your fault," she blubbered, "I was there too. I think we're both culpable."

"You could have come in through the front door, really,"

"I didn't want to see your sister or your parents," she said as she removed the jacket and held it out to me. I retrieved hers from the edge of the bed.

As we exchanged jackets, I updated Suzy on my family situation. She wasn't surprised that Laura was married and pregnant but when she learned Mom was dead she gasped, "Oh my God, I didn't know!"

"It's okay, calm down!" I said. I put my jacket on like it would stop me from bawling. I couldn't remember if Suzy's parents were at the funeral, but that whole day had been an awful blur. "Mom didn't suffer," I said quickly.

Suzy buried her face in her jacket and continued to cry so I gently steered her into my desk chair then went looking for tissue so she could blow her nose. Not finding any I grabbed a roll of toilet paper. "Here, use this," I said, handing her the roll. "You're getting tears and boogers all over your high school years."

She took the roll and looked at me as she asked wryly, "Toilet paper?"

"It's all I could find on short notice. I think the government has put a moratorium on the production of tissue."

Suzy blew her nose and then looked for a place to toss the used tissue. I grabbed the over-flowing wastepaper basket and held it out to her. She gave me a funny look.

"Working on something particularly challenging?" she asked.

"I was working on a letter of apology to you."

"Letter of apology?" Suzy let out a snort. "You mean for outing me to my parents and getting me kicked out of the family? You think a letter will do it?"

I flinched and drew back. "Hey!" I yelped. "Are you blaming me for that? I'm sorry, okay?"

"You're blaming yourself!" Suzy pointed out, looking at me incredulously.

"I wanted my jacket back. It's one of the few gifts my mother gave me that I liked, and it's pretty much all I have left of her," my voice trembled with emotion.

Suzy's eyes went wide and her face fell. "Oh God, I'm sorry! I shouldn't have said that!" she stammered, reaching for me. "I was trying to be funny!"

I stepped back. "How the hell did you keep that aspect of your life from your parents for so long?" I demanded. "I know you've done that before,"

Suzy raised her eyebrows. "That?" she repeated incredulously. "Can you even say the word?" she looked bewildered.

"I don't think it would have happened if we hadn't been drunk," I said quickly. "I'm sorry if I took advantage of you."

Suzy covered her face with her jacket and started shaking. I thought she was crying hysterically and I started to apologize again more profusely, then Suzy looked up revealing she wasn't crying but laughing.

"Oh Morgan, thank you for that! That's the funniest thing I've heard in a long time!" She laughed so hard she started braying like a donkey.

"Glad I could provide some levity," I was relieved, yet confused.

Suzy, fighting a smile, asked "Did I... take advantage of you?"

"I don't know," I admitted.

Suzy's eyes went wider. "You're blushing!" There was a pause then Suzy burst out with "Oh my God it was your first time wasn't it?"

"Yes, ma'am."

"Are you going to ask me if it was good for me?" Suzy cackled.

"If I have to ask, it probably wasn't," I said, remembering something I read in a women's magazine.

Suzy looked highly amused. "Should I ask if it was good for you?"

"I can honestly say it was the best I've ever had." I replied. "But I'm sorry I had to be drunk to attempt the maneuver."

"The maneuver?" she repeated incredulously. "Are you in ROTC by any chance? We made love, we did not storm the beach at Normandy!"

"I thought being drunk is a loser move?" I challenged.

Suzy got to her feet. "Morgan − are you drunk now?" she asked, a gleam in her eye.

I was confused. "What? No, I'm not drunk now."

Suzy raised her eyebrows. "Neither am I," she said, grinning and taking a step closer to me.

It slowly dawned on me what she was saying. "Oh!"

"At ease, soldier," she said, reaching for me.

When I opened my eyes it was morning and Suzy was in my arms. We were in my twin bed.

She was still asleep and had a big smile on her face. I felt very strong, protective and grown up. I kissed the top of her head tenderly. Suzy stirred, and then her eyelids fluttered. She looked at me.

"Good morning," she murmured softly. "How did you sleep?"

"I slept well. And you?" I asked gently, stroking her hair with my left hand.

"I slept well too — am I killing your arm?" Suzy asked, shifting slightly.

"I'm fine," I smiled.

Suzy rolled over so we were face to face. She ran her eyes over my body as she said, "Wow, you are really buff — your arms, your shoulders — everything!"

"I spend a lot of time in the weight room," I said. Compared to Suzy I was a monster. "You're so...so... lean," I said. "I'm afraid I'm going to break you. You had better be on top from now on."

Suzy looked incredulous. "From now on?" she repeated as she rolled on top of me straddling my hips. "Is this what you had in mind?" she asked as she started bouncing.

I was surprised. "Is this like the control experiment, you know, to make sure we got it right?" I meant it to be a joke but Suzy didn't take it that way.

Suzy stopped and the humor left her face. "Experiment? Is that what this is? Am I a lab rat to you?" she asked, with more than a hint of anger in her voice.

"Not at all," I stammered. "I'm new to this and I don't know what the protocol is?"

"Protocol..." she muttered, looking annoyed as she climbed out of bed and started to dress.

I sensed I had offended her. "I'm sorry," I said automatically.

Suzy let out a noise of exasperation. "Oh, for the love of God, Morgan, please stop apologizing!"

"Calm down!" I rolled out of bed and reached for my clothes. "Why are you so angry? I thought we ---"

"You thought wrong!" Suzy interrupted.

"Good to know," I said, trying to keep the hurt off my face and out of my voice and I don't think I succeeded because Suzy just sort of sighed and her face softened.

"Morgan, it was what it was, and that's all it was," she said tiredly. "Don't make it more than that,"

"I'm not." I said, but I wasn't sure what she meant.

Suzy glanced at me, then turned her attention back to getting dressed, looking in the mirror to comb her hair with her fingers as she said "I have to get going. My parents are giving me a two-hour window to get whatever I want from my room, then I am gone for good." She tossed me a look.

"How many times do you want me to say I'm sorry?" I bristled.

"I am not blaming you!" Suzy shot back.

"Yes, you are," I cried. "Don't put that on me!"

"I'm not!" she growled. "I saved your ass, by the way! My father tried to call your folks to out you, but the number was disconnected. I told him they had moved. Apparently the Gourmet Group broke up a few months back -- my folks are none the wiser."

She looked at me like she expected me to thank her, but I didn't.

Suzy grabbed her backpack from the floor and started stuffing the contents that had spilled on the floor back into the bag. She did it with such force you would have thought the underwear had insulted her.

"I hope they haven't thrown all my stuff out on the front lawn," she muttered.

"That would be kind of stupid of them. You're the only child they have left, remember?"

Suzy froze and stared at me in the mirror. Her eyes hardened as she hissed, "I cannot believe you just said that! Don't you ever say that again!"

"That's what you told me!" I reminded her, not sure why she was taking offense.

"You deal with your family, I'll deal with mine," she snapped. She shouldered the backpack. "Goodbye, Flynn," she said, the use of my last name letting me know she was angry.

"Goodbye Mathews. Good luck with your life." I replied.

Suzy's eyes narrowed, and she sort of shook her head then she grabbed her jacket from off the floor — double checked to make sure it was the right one — then stomped down the hall and out the front door, slamming it behind her. From the second-floor window over the landing I watched her head down the front walkway toward her car, the same one she drove in high school. She jerked it into gear and peeled out.

CHAPTER 11

Back to the Routine

A week later I was back at school preparing for field hockey practice. The team practiced every Sunday on the multipurpose pitch behind the football stadium. I always got there an hour early to warm up. Practice usually consisted of a few team drills followed by a scrimmage with half of the women dressed in black (the Goths) the others wearing brightly colored shirts (the Rainbows). North State University used to have a collegiate team and played in a league, but it was cut for financial reasons the year before I arrived on campus. Despite this, I took my goalie gear to college because I still wanted to play. I tossed a few balls onto the pitch and started running footwork drills, followed by wind sprints.

"Aren't you a dedicated player!"

I looked up to see Gator walking toward me with her silver and black stick over her shoulder.

Gator was 5'10" and looked every bit like a defensive player — she had a stocky body and long legs. Gator had more energy than most people. She worked several jobs both on and off campus and still managed to carry a full course load. I admired her greatly for this.

"Hey, Gator," I replied, then dispatched an orange practice ball into the wooden backstop with a vicious kick.

"Well, you're full of energy today," Gator observed. "Should I ask if you still have a crush on me?"

I stopped mid-kick and leveled a glare at her. "I don't," I said, although truth be told I wasn't sure how I felt. Between Gator and Suzy rebuffing me I figured romance and relationships were not something I was wired for. I went back to kicking the balls with such force they ricocheted off the backstop hard and high.

The rest of the team started to show up. Practices were led by Britany and Liam, the team captain and coach respectively. Both were professors at North State. They had immigrated from Scotland as undergrads. They both had blonde, almost white hair. I thought they looked more like brother and sister than husband and wife.

Everyone except for me came with either a black shirt and a primary-colored shirt, to be either a Goth or Rainbow. We often had new players join us for a practice or two, so practice always began with us in a circle each saying our names. Just about everyone had a nickname, because Britany said they were easier to remember than given names. It didn't take much to get a nickname. Fireball always wore orange and had a fiery temper. Spot always wore a polka-dotted bandanna. You get the idea. I was Wolf because at the first team practice I shared Dad's joke about me being raised by wolves until the age of four. I also tended to growl when the goal was charged. It bothered me a little that I didn't know most of my teammate's real names although we had been playing together for months, but I felt their nicknames suited them.

Every time someone charged the goal, I saw Suzy Mathews. I wasn't sure what to think about what had happened. I had outed her to her parents and probably ruined her life. The sex was okay (maybe — I had nothing to compare it to) but it bothered me that we had to be drunk. I wasn't sure if I had made love to Suzy or cheap champagne my first time, and the second round confused me.

During one play, I collided with Gator so hard she went down, getting a pretty good scrape on her right elbow. She looked at it, then scowled at me. "Take it easy! We're on the same side!"

"Sorry," I said automatically, although part of me was happy I had hurt her.

After practice some of the team stayed around to socialize but I had to hurry home to shower and change. Sunday afternoons I had my lab requirement for Intermediate Broadcasting. I was learning to be a radio producer as part of the Women's Radio Collective. The Collective consisted of five women who created and produced public affairs shows once a week. That day we were recording a program about the challenges of balancing parenthood and college. Gator, who was ostensibly training me, was going to conduct the interviews while I ran the recording equipment in the production studio.

I lived in the converted attic of a house about a mile from campus. I lived by myself because I had a bad experience with roommates earlier in the year. It was Dad's idea that I find a place of my own and he announced he would cover the rent, as long as I covered everything else. It came with a kitchen table, two chairs and that was it for furnishings. I had lived there for about a month, and the only furniture I added was a bookcase made from a collection of stolen milk crates and wooden planks. I slept on the floor in a pile of sheets, blankets, and my Girl Scout sleeping bag. I was saving up for a bed.

My only income came from a part-time job delivering the college newspaper. For this I earned the princely cash sum of $40 a week. I lived carefully and cheaply. Most of the time I didn't run the heat in my place. I stole toilet paper from the dispensers on campus. I ate ramen noodles, vegetables, and peanut butter and jelly pretty much every day. The only time I drove my car, a 1983 Ford sedan, was when I went grocery shopping or getting to and from hockey practice because I had to haul the goalie gear. Usually I rode my bike to school.

"Hello Morgan, how was your break?" Ramona, the unofficial leader of the Women's Radio Collective, greeted me when I walked in to the radio station. She had the afternoon board operator shift.

"I'm glad to be back," I answered truthfully.

Gator arrived, freshly showered, wearing khakis and a button-down shirt with her burgundy Lacoste jacket. She looked like she was going on a date. I was in my usual jeans, hooded sweatshirt and white high-top sneakers. I wondered if I should have dressed up more. Gator was holding something behind her back. She grinned at me, then brought out my field hockey stick.

"What are you doing with my stick?" I asked, surprised.

"You left it on the pitch under the bleachers," Gator gave me a scolding look. Forgetting your stick was right up there with leaving the baby on the bus.

"Oh! Thanks for grabbing it," Embarrassed, I took the stick and laid it against the wall by the table.

Gator lifted her elbow so I could see the scrape. She had put a bandage on it, but you could still see that it was ugly. She gave me a look. "Are you sure you don't still have a crush on me?"

I stepped away from her. "I don't even like you as a person, Gator," I snapped.

Gator drew back. "Whoa! That was hostile!" she gasped, blanching.

I went over to the cabinet that held the microphones and cords. I kept my back to her as I asked "Could we please just stay on task? How many guests are we expecting today?"

"Three if they all show up," Gator said, all business. "And I'll be in the studio with them asking the questions."

"Okay, four mics it is," I said, grabbing what we needed.

I had just finished setting up the studio when the guests, a man and two women arrived. Gator escorted them to the studio where she would interview them. They all had children who used the school's onsite daycare. They would talk about the convenience of having that on campus and if it wasn't there, they couldn't take classes.

I watched with admiration as Gator, her voice smooth as honey, kept the guests on topic and engaged. I scribbled notes furiously because I wanted to keep track of the places where people said something poignant, which we could use for the promos, or when people stumbled, so we would have a better idea where the edits needed to be. The interview went over an hour but the program could not be longer than a forty-five minutes. We had editing time on Monday and Thursday evenings, so the next night the Collective was back in the studio. It was also our weekly meeting where we pitched ideas for upcoming programs.

It was warm with all of us in the room, so I peeled off my sweatshirt. I was wearing my FIELD HOCKEY GOALIES ARE HARD TO KILL t-shirt. It was a Christmas gift from Dad. It was red, and on the back was an illustration of a goalie exploding out of the cage and through a crowd of offensive players.

Gator showed off her damaged elbow, saying it was the perfect shirt for me. Ramona laughed, then sort of started like she just remembered something. She left the room and came back a moment later with my field hockey stick. "You left this in the station yesterday. I hid it behind the record stacks so I could give it to you tonight," she explained.

Gator made a noise of surprise, looking at me incredulously as she burst out with, "That's the second time you've forgotten your stick! What's wrong with you?"

"I guess I'm a little distracted lately," I stammered, blushing.

Gator grinned. "You're a lot distracted! Is she cute?"

I closed my eyes, cringing while they laughed. When I opened my eyes they were all staring at me. "I think I need a lap," I squeaked.

"I think we all need a break," Ramona announced. "Everybody here is getting low blood sugar. I'll tell you what, me and Kathy are going to head to the Quickie Mart across the bridge and get some snacks. Be back in fifteen minutes?" Kathy was Ramona's girlfriend who chose the music for the shows.

"Got it," I said, glancing at the clock, then I headed out the door. Running always made me feel better. I sprinted out of the building and headed up the hill to the football field and track. One lap around the track and then I would head back to the station at a dead run. Sometimes when I ran, I would imagine being chased by whatever was bothering me. The faster I ran, the farther it was behind me.

Gator was sitting on one of the stools behind the reel-to-reel machine, still working dutifully when I came roaring into the production studio.

"She's back!" Gator greeted me. "Feel better?"

I nodded, gulping air and prancing like a horse to cool down.

Gator glanced at the clock. "Ramona and Kathy should be back in a few."

I nodded, suddenly getting a chill so I put my sweatshirt back on and pulled the hood up over my head.

Gator looked at me. "Did something happen during winter break?" she asked carefully. "You've forgotten your stick twice and you have a look on your face like you're thinking about something ...or someone? Did something happen?"

"Yeah," I said sadly, surprising myself when I blurted out "Suzy happened."

"Oh!" Gator exclaimed. There was a pause, then she asked,

"Who is Suzy?"

"Someone I grew up with. We were the Tomboys of Cherry Lane."

"Oh dear! This sounds serious," Gator remarked reproachfully. "I take it you saw her over winter break?"

I nodded. "I did, and I think it was a mistake."

Gator gave me a worried look. "How big of a mistake? Was it a 'I have to find a lawyer now' type of mistake?"

I stared at her, puzzled. "I don't think so? What is the age of consent for a lesbian relationship?"

Gator's eyes went wide.

"Eighteen is the age of consent. How old are you? How old is she?"

"I'm twenty. She's twenty-five."

Gator sighed with relief. "You're both legal. I take it consenting took place?" she asked, a gleam in her eye as she used finger quotes on the word consenting. Before I could answer, Gator addressed the ceiling as she cried dramatically, "Oh my God, please tell me she did not get you pregnant!"

"Is that even possible?"

I have no idea how Gator kept from laughing as she said, "Oh sure! *'Lesbians Can Conceive,'* that will be the title of my first book." Then she got an evil grin as she added, "You wouldn't believe the positions!"

"Are you serious?" I was completely perplexed.

Gator bit back a smile. "No, parthenogenesis is not a thing — at least not yet."

"Good to hear," I sighed.

Gator looked troubled as she asked "Is she straight? Did she experiment with you?"

"No," I shook my head. "She's one of us. She plays field hockey."

"What position?"

"Forward, mostly wing."

Gator made a face. "Oh! She plays offense! I'm so sorry!"

"Thank you. She's really skinny – I'm talking she's a gazelle. If anyone was going to do the impregnating, it probably would have been me. She's way too fem to impregnate anything." I said savagely.

That made Gator laugh. "Of course! You do play defense, after all! And Lord knows we defense girls are rough and ready!" she declared, throwing her arm around my shoulders.

I stiffened. "What are you doing?"

"I am attempting to comfort you," Gator explained patiently. "This is the jock hug — you only use one arm. Now unclench your fists... relax your shoulders... there you go! See? Not so bad. Congratulations! Welcome to the tribe!"

"I don't know how to feel about this," I said, permitting the embrace. "I feel like I'm going through puberty again!"

"Of course you are! You don't get to go through it at the normal time when you're gay!" Gator cried, releasing me.

I looked at her. "How old were you when you finally went through puberty?"

Gator looked thoughtful. "Second year of college. Some girl pulled the fake sleep move on me."

I'd heard about this move. It's when you're sleeping next to another woman and she pretends to be asleep and puts her arm around you.

"I've never had the fake sleep move pulled on me," I said.

"The fake sleep move is not a requirement to be a member of the tribe." Gator said gently. "You don't have to be physical to be one of the girls."

We finished editing by nine o'clock and Gator insisted on giving me a ride home, putting my bike into the back of her truck. She even carried it up the stairs to the apartment. As she wheeled it in she sort of looked around then remarked, "You don't have a bed!"

"Yeah? So?"

Gator's expression softened a bit as she asked, "Do you want a bed?"

"Yeah, I just don't have the money yet," I explained, embarrassed. "Please don't tell anyone."

Gator saw the pain on my face and stopped smiling.

"I won't. I'm sorry, I didn't mean to pry or give you grief. I was just asking because I work part-time doing deliveries for a furniture company with my truck. Sometimes they damage stuff out — that means they can't sell it because it has a cosmetic defect, so they sort of offer it to employees for a significantly reduced price. If a bed comes up, would you be interested?"

"Yeah!" I brightened. "That would be great!"

"Okay," Gator smiled, then looking at my make-shift bookcase, remarked "Wow, look at that – Fitzgerald, Hemingway, Steinbeck, Mark Twain. You sure like the classics! If I can get a bookcase would you like that too?"

I nodded, then sort of shoved my hands in my pockets and squirmed as I said, "Please don't tell anyone I don't have a bookcase either."

Gator made a dismissive gesture.

"I won't say a word," she promised.

CHAPTER 12

Surprises

Gator kept her word, and a week later I was the proud owner of a full-size futon mattress and a slightly damaged pine frame. I pulled money from my savings account for the down payment. The rest would be paid in increments of at least $25 a month. A few days after the futon was in use Gator said she had a bookcase that had been left behind in one of the apartments she managed. She would bring it over on Sunday morning then give me a ride to practice.

I was in my practice clothes when Gator, dressed in her sweats, proudly marched up the stairs, carrying one of the shelves over her head like a hunter returning with a fresh kill.

"Behold! I bring you storage for your sacred texts!" Gator announced dramatically. "The rest of it is in the truck," she said, placing the shelf off to the side.

The bookcase was awkward as we carried it through the alley and up the stairs.

"Where do you want it?" Gator asked as we maneuvered it through the door.

"Main room," I grunted.

"Your books are going to look good in this!" Gator beamed as we put it down. "What are you going to do with the planks and milk crates?"

I looked at my makeshift bookshelves. "I don't know," I shrugged.

"What about turning the old bookcase into a platform for your bed?" Gator suggested. "It would get you higher off the floor and away from drafts, and it would also give you some additional storage space."

"I like that idea," I said, and with Gator's help I unstacked the bookcase. We arranged the milk crates and planks into a frame, then put the futon on top of the planks so the frame was now fourteen inches off the floor, afterwards Gator helped me make the bed. As we put the comforter on, she suggested I try the bed out to make sure it was stable. I sat down on the edge of the futon. It creaked a little as I swung my legs on to the mattress, and then rolled over onto my stomach to look at her.

"It seems okay," I said.

Gator got a wicked smile. "Aw, Morgan, you look like a cute little centerfold," she teased, then burst out laughing when I scrambled to my feet like the futon had suddenly turned into a nest of cobras.

I glanced at my watch. "Gee, we need to get to practice!"

"Let's go!" Gator shouted, heading down the stairs.

I tended goal for the Goths for the first half of the game. The Rainbows got one past me, but I stopped three before Liam blew the whistle for halftime water break.

I was standing with my back to the parking lot and had my helmet on the back of my head, as I drank from my water bottle when Liam sort of looked past me and smiled and waved.

"Everyone! We have a new player! Everyone, this is Zan," Liam said, waving her into the group. "She's new to NSU."

I glanced over my shoulder and nearly jumped out of my skin. Zan was Suzy! I gagged and did a spit-take, surprising Gator and Spot who were on either side of me.

"Well, that was festive!" Gator remarked as I sort of stumbled and coughed. She gave me a funny look. "You okay?"

I pulled my helmet back on. Suddenly I was shaking all over.

"I'm cold," I lied as I started jogging in place.

Suzy sort of nodded to the team as she walked up and apologized for being late.

"I had to hunt around for my pitch sneakers," she said. "I just moved here and I'm living out of boxes. I couldn't find my stick, but I know I packed it."

"We have extras," said Britany, reaching for the club stick bag. She asked what brought Suzy to NSU.

"I'm here short-term," Suzy said, "for one semester, to finish up my master's degree. I was just hired at the San Francisco Aquarium and they're paying for it. We're installing a North Coast exhibit, and I'll be in charge of it."

"Welcome Zan," Britany said, handing her one of the spare sticks. "Is Zan short for something?"

"Short for Suzanne." Suzy explained, weighing the stick in her hand as she looked over the team. "I played for the University of California and the U.S. Olympic team," she said as if issuing a challenge.

"Wonderful. Since you're all in black you can play with the Goths today," Liam said. "We play Goths versus Rainbows."

Suzy raised her eyebrows. "How's that?"

"Black-clad players against those in bright colors." Britany explained helpfully. "Ergo, Goths versus Rainbows. Each player brings a black shirt and a colored shirt to practice."

"That's cute," Suzy smirked. She didn't show any recognition toward me, but as I was standing in profile and with all the gear I had on, I figured she didn't recognize me. I racked my brain, trying to remember if I had told her I was at North State -- it seemed that I would have, but I figured she'd been so drunk she probably didn't remember it.

We went around the circle one more time so Suzy could learn our names. When my turn came I said, "Wolf" in a howl which made everyone laugh and Gator said her name in a guttural growl which also got a chuckle. Suzy reacted to both with sort of a weird look, and I wondered if she was reminded of high school and the Wildcat growl.

The game resumed. I was now tending goal for the Rainbows and I pulled Gator, who was my sweep, onto the pitch "Let's go!"

"What's going on?" Gator asked.

I turned around so my back was toward the rest of the team. "That new woman? Zan? That's Suzy!"

Gator's eyes nearly bugged out of her head. "Oh shit! Are you serious? Suzy? As in Winter Break Suzy?"

"Yes!" my voice cracked.

Gator looked up the field. "She doesn't look too scary. Why didn't you say hi to her?"

"It's too weird!" I squeaked.

"Do you mean weird because you -ahem- consented?" Gator leered.

"It was more than that," I said, blushing. "Right after we consented her parents walked in on us and it outed her. Then she showed up at my house that night because they kicked her out of the house, and we consented again then had a big fight the next morning."

Gator's eyes went even wider. "Oh, good God, Morgan! Way to bury the lede! That is the Queen Mother of weird!" she looked over her shoulder. "I don't think she recognized you."

"I'm sure she didn't, the helmet got in the way," I agreed, glad I was on my second set of goalie gear since high school so Suzy didn't recognize it. "What do I do? How do I handle this?"

Gator shot a furtive look up field.

"Keep the helmet on!" she ordered, then she rolled her eyes skyward as she muttered, "Dear Lord, please don't let me slip up and call you Morgan today!"

Liam blew the whistle calling the game back into play. The Goths got the ball quickly and swarmed the goal. Suzy was playing forward, and she had that look of grim determination on her face that I knew so well. I growled as I came out of the cage which surprised her, and she sort of drew up short as I tackled the ball and cleared it off to the side.

Suzy gave me a funny look as she retrieved the ball I had kicked out of bounds.

"What's with the growling?" she asked Parrot, the midfielder with hair dyed red and blue.

"That's Wolf, that's what she does," Parrot replied. "It's the song of her people."

Suzy sort of shook her head as play resumed.

Finally, Liam glanced at his watch and blew the whistle indicating practice was over.

Suzy was surprised to learn no one had bothered to keep score. "If you don't keep score, how do you know if your game is improving?" she asked.

"We're about fun and skills, not scoring," Britany explained. "But we're mostly about having fun."

Suzy looked at Britany like she had announced we routinely sacrificed a goat on the pitch.

I was always one of the last to leave because I had to pack up my gear. Bootsy, so named because she wore Wellingtons as fashion, hung around because she had a project in the works with Fireball and they needed to discuss it. Gator who was my ride, helped me with the gear bag. Suzy seemed reluctant to leave. She was holding on to the stick she borrowed from Britany as she sort of looked everyone over then remarked, "You guys are the strangest field hockey team I've ever met."

"How's that?" Fireball asked, arching an eyebrow.

Suzy shook her head. "I've played field hockey since high school. I played in college, and I was first alternate for the US Olympic women's team. I have never played a match where we didn't keep score." Then she glanced at me, as she added, "and I have never played on a team where the goalie growled like some sort of beast, and everyone had silly nicknames. I guess it is funny and all, but it's like something a bunch of boys would do on the playground. What's wrong with just trying to be a better player?"

That was quite a speech, and so loaded with disdain that even Bootsy, who prided herself on being a non-violent Buddhist, had her hackles raised.

"What's wrong with the nicknames?" she asked stiffly. "They're fun. What's wrong with Wolf growling? I like it. It lets me know she means business!"

"What kind of a name is Wolf anyway?" Suzy asked, looking at me askance.

"My Native American name." I said seriously.

I still had the helmet on so Suzy couldn't totally see my face, but I did see a flicker of recognition in her eyes, but before she could say anything, Gator chimed in with, "I've got news for you, little girl, Wolf gets out here a good forty-five minutes to an hour before the rest of us and runs drills. Most of us practice on our own too. So don't be trying to tell us that we don't want to be better players."

Suzy blinked. "Little girl?" she repeated.

"Everyone is little to me." Gator quipped, tossing a look at Fireball. They both towered over Suzy by at least five inches.

"I sense I have offended," Suzy stammered, glancing nervously between Fireball and Gator.

"Yeah, you did," Fireball said, looking at the rest of us. We nodded in agreement.

"I'm sorry you took it that way," Suzy replied gruffly. "I guess I'm old-school, but I think the nicknames and growling are antithetical to the grace of the sport."

"Antithetical?" Bootsy asked, throwing a look at Gator who was a walking dictionary.

"It means directly opposed to something," Gator replied, giving Suzy a look of disdain.

"Nicknames are easy to remember," said Fireball. "That's why camp counselors have them."

"I don't think I've ever had a nickname," Suzy countered, letting us know she wasn't buying the explanation.

"Sure you have," I said. Out of the corner of my eye I saw Gator's head whip around because she heard the challenge in my voice as I continued, "You were known as Suzy as a child. That's a nickname. And when you got a bit older, some called you Suze."

"Do... I know you?" Suzy asked, her eyes narrowing like a cat's in front of a mouse hole.

I continued removing the gear as I said "It's the classic progression of the name Suzanne. The diminutive when you are younger, and then there is an attempt to move away from the diminutive as you mature."

"Oh," Suzy relaxed a little. "I guess that makes sense?" She cocked her head, and then asked with forced cheerfulness, "Let me guess: you're a psychology major?"

Then I went in for the kill as I said, "Then there was that other nickname, the one you got when you coached the high school field hockey team. The older girls called you Traffic Ticket because they said you had 'fine' written all over you."

The color increased in Suzy's face, and she looked positively stunned as she demanded "How do you know I coached the high school team?"

I yanked the helmet off. "Hello, Suzy." I grinned a grin that Gator described as the kind of grin sharks have when they come across prey. "And about the growling - have you forgotten the Wildcat growl? You taught it to me. It was cultural."

"Morgan!" Suzy cried. "What are you doing here?" She looked surprised and happy to see me.

"Getting an education," I replied.

Gator bit back a smile.

Bootsy and Fireball exchanged a look, then Bootsy, who I swear could be calm if she was being attacked by bees, asked, "Do you two know each other?"

"Yep," I said, removing the rest of the gear and packing it in the bag. "We grew up together."

Suzy laughed until she started to cough. "I didn't know you were going to school here! Did you tell me?"

"Maybe." I shrugged. "There was a lot going on." I looked at Gator. "Ready to go, Gator?"

"Yep," Gator nodded. "Let's go."

I grabbed one end of the goalie bag and gestured for Gator to grab the handle on the other end.

We started toward the parking lot.

"Wait!" Suzy cried, walking briskly to keep up with us. "Can I get your phone number at least? So we can talk?"

Talk? I wondered. Gator gave me a 'that could be good' look, but I blurted out "We really need to go — Gator and I have to get work — I'll see you around. We'll catch up later, okay?"

We drove off, leaving Suzy standing in the parking lot, holding the borrowed stick and looking stunned — and a little annoyed.

As we turned out of the parking lot Gator said tiredly "Morgan, you need to talk to her."

"I do?"

"God yes!" She gave me a scolding look as she said, "There's something unfinished there, and it's going to get worse if you don't address it."

"I don't know what," I argued. "She said it was what it was. It didn't mean anything,"

Gator shook her head. "I'm not buying it," she scoffed. "From her reaction and your reaction there is something. An uncomfortable something." She glanced at me as she added reproachfully, "You seem more hurt than angry."

I bristled. "She should be angry with me! I outed her to her parents. We were both drunk after a memorial service. It wouldn't have happened otherwise."

"You didn't mention the memorial service," Gator's voice rose. "This sounds like trauma bonding."

"What's that?"

Gator proceeded to explain the false sense of closeness that happens when you share a traumatic experience with other people.

"It's not real, but it sure feels like it is," she said. "It can make you do all sorts of stupid things.

"We're looking at stupid in the rearview mirror," I groused. "I don't know what to say to her."

Gator sighed. "Maybe just listen to what she wants to say? Morgan, physical intimacy doesn't necessarily mean emotional intimacy, but it varies from person to person. It may have been nothing to you, but she still wants to talk."

I shook my head. "It doesn't seem real now. When I'm home, what happens at college doesn't seem real, and now that I'm here, what happened at home doesn't seem real."

"That's kind of a big disconnect," Gator replied, looking troubled. "That's compartmentalizing to the nth degree! You might want to work on that."

"Okay," I said. We drove the rest of the way in silence.

CHAPTER 13

Birthday Presents

The next day I ran into Bootsy on campus. She told me she walked home from practice with Suzy because, as it turned out, they both lived in the same giant apartment complex two blocks off campus. Suzy recognized Bootsy from an advanced biology class they had together and struck up a conversation which included asking for my telephone number.

"I lied and told her I didn't have it," Bootsy said, looking troubled. "There's something dark about her." Bootsy explained that Liam had recruited Suzy for the team. "She's in one of his classes and when he noticed the UC Santa Cruz Field Hockey pin on her backpack, he invited her to join."

"Wonderful," I rolled my eyes. "Remind me to slam into Liam on the pitch next time we practice, won't you?"

"I can do that," Bootsy nodded, then abruptly changed the subject by asking me about my upcoming birthday. "You're turning twenty-one on Friday! That's a big birthday!" Bootsy kept track of everyone's birthday on the team. "Gator and Fireball want to take you out on the town. Everyone who is of age will be there. But first you need to get an ear cuff." She pulled back her hair so I could see the silver band clipped to right ear. Bootsy had her twenty-first birthday in November.

"Why do I need an ear cuff?" I asked. Jewelry was never my thing.

Bootsy shrugged. "It's an athletic girl thing. You get it on your 21st birthday."

"Where do I get one? And how much do these cost? Money is kind of tight right now."

Bootsy waved dismissively. "Don't worry about that. How about if we meet you on the steps of the library at three o'clock today?"

"Okay?" I shrugged, noting the mischievous gleam in her eyes. "What a minute, who is 'we'?"

Bootsy grinned. "Don't worry, you're gonna like it. We'll see you then," and she scampered off.

"Who is 'we'?" I called after her. Bootsy just waved and kept going.

That day Gator sat in front of me in Journalism History. I guess she wasn't terribly interested in the lecture, because in the middle of it a note was dropped on my desk.

"Did Suzy catch up with you? Ran into her this morning at KNSU. She heard your voice on the radio this morning and came looking for you." Gator wrote.

"Heard my voice?" I wrote back, a chill coming over me.

"Yeah. I worked the morning shift at the station this morning and ran the promo for the afternoon newscast — you know the

one with all the reporters introducing themselves?" Gator wrote. *"I told her she wasn't allowed to be in the station unless she worked there, and she left."* That was a bald-faced lie on Gator's part, but I appreciated it all the same.

"Thanks for protecting me." I replied.

"I'm your sweeper, that's what I do."

That afternoon I was sitting on the steps of the library right as Bootsy and Fireball walked up with impish looks on their faces.

"Happy birthday, Wolf!" they cried as one, and Fireball very proudly handed me a small red velvet bag with a gold silk tassel drawstring. Inside the bag was a copper ear cuff with dimpled finish. It was beautiful and Bootsy looked very pleased as she put it on my right ear.

"I designed it. Fireball made it." she beamed. "We were supposed to give it to you on Sunday, but it wasn't done," she tossed a look at Fireball who smirked and nodded sheepishly.

"It's gorgeous!" I exclaimed. "Thanks, guys!" I said, my voice thick with emotion.

"You're welcome, Wolfie," Fireball embraced me in the jock hug. "Happy birthday!"

I felt good as I headed off to my shift in the KNSU newsroom. I wrote and anchored the Monday afternoon newscasts. My favorite part was when I heard the trumpet fanfare for National Public Radio's *All Things Considered* in my left ear and the person running the board in my right ear counting me down to the end of the last newscast. There was such a sense of accomplishment when I got it timed perfectly. Today was one of those days.

As I was leaving the studio the guy running the sound board let me know Gator had called from the journalism department office. Gator worked in the office on Monday afternoons. A box addressed to me had been delivered there. The house, right across the street from the radio station, was officially known as Bret Harte House, named for an American short-story writer and journalist who came through the area in the 1850s. It was a three-story home that had been built in the early 1900s. The university took it over in the 1940s when the university expanded. It still had hardwood floors and pane glass windows. I liked it because it had a wood stove and was always warm.

I shivered when I got outside and was glad I only had to go across a street. North State was right on the coast and always had a damp cold, but that unpleasantness was tempered with the smell of salt air and spruce trees. It was a day I should have been wearing the wool peacoat Mom bought me when I started college, but since she died the coat made me too sad, so I stuffed it in the closet and wore multiple sweatshirts instead. Dad had reclaimed his Marine jacket years before.

"There you are! We have a box for you!" Gator announced. The normally busy office was empty except for the two of us. The only sound was KNSU playing on a radio behind the receptionist's desk.

"A box for me?" I asked. "What is it?"

"Don't know, didn't open it," Gator said, gesturing to the large white cardboard box that sat on the coffee table. "It's from your father."

"I wonder why he sent it here?" I mused as I sat down on the couch.

Gator handed me scissors to open the box. Inside, wrapped up in green tissue paper was my letterman jacket. After the incident with Suzy, I had stuffed the jacket into the back of my closet — I hadn't told Dad about what happened — was he sending me a message?

I dropped the box and jumped away from it so abruptly I startled Gator.

"What is it?" she cried, leaping out from behind the desk. She grabbed the box and her brow furrowed as she pulled the jacket out by one shoulder. "It's a letterman jacket?" she said, giving me a funny look. She held it up and turned it around slowly. "And by the looks of it...it's yours?"

"I see that," I said, and my voice cracked. "I left it at home because Mom didn't want me to take it to college."

A white envelope fell out of the jacket. Gator picked it up.

"It's addressed to you," she said, handing it to me.

I took a seat on the couch. Inside the envelope was a check for $300 and a letter from Dad. *"Dear Morgan, I can hardly believe that on March 15, 21 years ago, you arrived. I am sending you this jacket on your 21st birthday as it is a most important birthday, and I want you to understand how priorities and goals change as we mature. There was a time when all you wanted was to letter in sports, get good grades, and get into college. Now that you are well into your college years, I have no doubt that your goals have evolved. What was once so important, like lettering in track or field hockey, may not be as important as it once was? Whatever goals you set, pursue them with dedication and ardor. I am sending you this jacket to keep you warm. I recall it took some* *effort to persuade your mother to allow you to have this jacket. I told her you needed something warm to wear, as the sweatshirts you often wore didn't cut it, and that your successes in academics and athletics needed to be recognized for the accomplishments they were. Although your mother did not want you to take this jacket to college, I insist you have it now. May this jacket keep you warm and remind you of how much I love you. P.S. I am sending along $300. Use it as you see fit — preferably to buy steak and fly! P.P.S. I sent this to the journalism department because I sent it certified mail and I wanted to be sure someone was there to sign for it. Love, Dad."*

By the time I got to the end of the letter I was blinking back tears.

"Is it a good letter?" Gator asked gently.

"Yeah," I sniffed. "He sent it to me for my birthday. Mom made me leave it at home."

Gator smiled as she held the jacket by the shoulders and scrutinized the patches. "Oh, my! You were quite the over-achiever, weren't you? Look at that! Field hockey! Track! Journalism!" She frowned. "Why didn't your mom want you to bring this to college with you? It's very clean, and it looks warm."

"Mom said it was inappropriate at college," I said, "and she was embarrassed and ashamed of her dumb jock dyke daughter."

Gator looked at me like I was crazy. "The last thing you are is dumb!" she scowled, adding, "This is a nice, warm jacket and I bet it looks great on you. Put it on, let me see what you look like in it."

I turned my back to Gator as I peeled off the sweatshirts and set them aside, then put on the jacket. It was like I was reclaiming it. After Suzy left my house that day, I was unsure if I would ever want to wear it again because it reminded me of her.

Gator was smiling as I turned around. "You look great." she said.

That night I called Dad to thank him. He responded by telling me that Suzy Mathews was now at North State finishing her master's degree. She called Dad at work looking for my contact information. She knew where Dad worked because he came to career day at the high school.

"Did you give it to her?" I asked.

"Yes, I did," Dad replied. "Is that a problem?"

"No, Dad, I just don't have a lot of time for socializing these days because I'm so busy with school." I lied. Dad didn't ask about the memorial or anything else from that weekend, so I was pretty sure he didn't have a clue about what went down. I hadn't told Dad I was gay and didn't really want to just yet.

"You need to make time for yourself and friends," he chided me. "It might be nice to see Suzy again. There's no friend like an old friend."

CHAPTER 14

Behind the Mask

*F*riday night my teammates who were over twenty-one took me out to dinner at DiBono's, the one and only fancy place in town. They were wearing their ear cuffs as a statement, and I wore mine too.

Dinner was followed by what Fireball called "an age-appropriate tour of the Northtown Plaza" which had a total of six bars in a four-block radius. They got me appropriately drunk, then took me home and put me to bed. I slept most of Saturday and was still a little hungover on Sunday, but I went to practice anyway because usually it was the best part of the week for me.

"Surprised you're here!" Gator teased.

"I hate you." I replied, making her laugh.

"You look hung," Suzy announced, then she frowned. "Was there a party last night?" She was dressed all in black again but had wisely brought a bright yellow shirt so she could play on the Rainbows team if needed.

"Friday night," Fireball grinned as she ruffled my hair. "This one turned twenty-one. We took her out on the town for an age-appropriate excursion."

"You took her bar hopping," Suzy groused, annoyed.

"It was kind of a last-minute thing," Gator lied.

"Sure it was. Birthdays are always last-minute things," Suzy growled, letting Gator know she didn't believe it for a second. She gave me a hard look. "Did you have a good time? Of course you did! You had a 24-hour hangover! Good job, Spunky!"

"Spunky?" The entire team repeated as one. They all looked at me with amusement, obviously awaiting an explanation.

"High school nickname, freshman year." I replied. "I was the smallest of the goalies and the goalie coach said what I lacked in size I made up for in spunk."

"She got into a fist fight at her first practice," Suzy said smugly. "And in the first grade she beat up three girls who called her a boy."

"After they jumped me," I said defensively. "It was three against one!"

Liam looked amazed. "Wow, you've been a scrapper since grammar school!" he sputtered.

"Certainly explains why she plays goalie," Britany said.

"We should have kicked you off the high school team," Suzy scowled.

"Thank goodness you didn't," Fireball interjected, drawing herself up to her full height as she shouted "Get into the cage, Spunky, I'm feeling spirited. Let's do this!"

I jogged on to the pitch dribbling a ball. Gator and Fireball moved with me, pushing balls with their sticks. Fireball rolled her eyes and mouthed the words, "What a bitch!"

I nodded in agreement then added, "Don't you dare call me Spunky again!"

"Understood," Fireball nodded.

"You got it, Spunky," Gator chirped.

Bootsy shot a furtive look at Suzy, who had gone up field passing a ball back and forth with a midfielder.

"Maybe we should have invited her," Bootsy muttered with a guilty look.

"Then I wouldn't have shown up," I groused. I still hadn't talked to her like Gator said I needed to. I think I was afraid to.

Suzy ended up playing for the Rainbows. When she got the ball, she kept it. She wasn't about passing to a teammate. The other players noticed this. When she took a shot, she lifted it. It was aggressive play, yet despite this I stopped two with my mitt — and only one got past me.

"You were fierce out there!" said Shark, who came from the East coast where they played for blood (hence her nickname) as she gave Suzy a stick tap as they walked off the pitch at the end of practice.

"Thanks," Suzy nodded, slightly out of breath. She didn't seem to notice the looks of annoyance she was getting from others on the team for the way she yelled instructions at them during play as if she was the coach.

As we gathered at the bleachers at the end of practice Britany announced, "Nobody leave yet! We have a surprise for you!" She nodded at Liam, who jogged to the parking lot then returned carrying a large white cardboard box with NSU stickers all over it. "Take a seat, ladies!" Britany grinned impishly as she gestured for us to sit down. "I have a good friend who captains a field hockey club in British Columbia," she began, "The team is going to do a West Coast tour and they agreed to stop here at NSU if we want to play an exhibition game against them. It will be three weeks from today. It would mean adding more practices. Are we interested?" she asked hopefully.

Everyone sort of looked at each other and smiled.

"A real game?" Shark asked. "With officials and everything?"

"Yes," Britany nodded. "Are we interested?" she repeated, her voice rising a bit.

"Yes!" I cried and the other women laughed and echoed the sentiment.

"I was hoping that would be the response!" Britany beamed, nodding to Liam. "If we're going to play as an official team, we need official uniforms."

Liam opened the box revealing a stack of green warm up jackets and gold short-sleeved shirts with NSU Field Hockey printed on them and kilts in a green and gold tartan.

"These are the uniforms from NSU back in the day," he said. "They were freshly laundered this week and now I present them to you. You ladies are going to look sharp for this game!"

Liam handed out jackets as Britany focused on kilts and shirts. The goalie jersey is always a different color than the team jersey and Britany reminded me of this as she handed me a bright red goalie jersey with a big number 1 on it.

Everyone was happy to see the uniforms, everyone that is, except Suzy who looked annoyed as she accepted a uniform size small.

"We shouldn't wear these," Suzy said sourly, holding up the kilt.

"Why not?" Fireball asked, as the entire team looked at Suzy. "They look okay."

"This is clan Gordon," Suzy said, then she went on to explain that she was Scottish on her father's side and had been to Scotland where she learned all about tartans. According to Suzy, wearing a tartan you were not entitled to by family lineage was an insult to the Scottish people.

Britany and Liam, both from Scotland, shared a look as if to say, 'no one told us about this', and Liam sort of stiffened as he said patiently, "It is the uniform of the university."

"We shouldn't be wearing it." Suzy repeated. "It's silly."

"Everything seems silly to you," I heard myself saying, "ever since that unfortunate incident."

"What incident?" Suzy asked suspiciously.

"That time you sat on your field hockey stick and it went up your butt — and stayed there!" I replied.

The team — except for Suzy — burst out laughing. Britany shot me a scolding look, shaking her head, then addressed Suzy. "Zan, speaking as a daughter of Scotland I can assure you, my people will not be offended by North State wearing traditional kit."

"It is the uniform," Liam repeated, this time in his coach voice.

That took the fun out of the moment and most of the team left quickly, with the exception of Suzy, who glared daggers at me as I packed up. Gator and Fireball, sensing the tension, stayed behind. When it was just the four of us, Suzy started in.

"You're so good with these little quips, Morgan, but I think it might be important for you to listen to someone else's opinion."

"And you think your opinion is the one that matters?" I asked acidly. "Quit talking down to me! I'm not fourteen-years-old anymore. You are not the coach. You are no longer in a position of authority."

"I realize that!" Suzy's voice rose, and she started to defend her position on the uniforms, but Fireball wouldn't have it.

"What is your major malfunction?" Fireball bellowed, making all of us jump and Suzy closed her mouth. Fireball got to her feet and glared at Suzy. "The kilt is the uniform of the NSU field hockey team! We are that team! We will wear the uniform!"

"It's not just the uniform!" Suzy cried. "I've played against those teams from British Columbia! They are serious! They practice every day! We're a bullshit club team from a podunk college wearing a tartan we have no right to wear, and even with extra practices they're going to wipe the floor with us!"

"Podunk college?" I repeated, stunned. "This podunk college is enabling you to get your dream job!"

"I'm doing my time and then I'm gone," Suzy replied in a tone usually reserved for serial killers.

"You're overreacting," Gator said curtly. "We play for fun."

"You can have fun but still take the game seriously!" Suzy shouted. "That growling thing you do, Morgan? That needs to stop. It was cute in high school but now it's an embarrassment."

"You must have a really high opinion of yourself to be so judgmental," I snarled.

"I'm trying to help you be a better player!" Suzy cried.

"I don't want your help! No one wants your help!" I answered angrily.

"And no one is forcing you to play," Fireball chimed in, throwing a look at Gator, who nodded.

They both looked cross.

Suzy looked surprised and she stepped back, like she just realized how big Gator and Fireball were. "I'm just trying to be helpful," she stammered.

"You're not helpful," I said tiredly. "If you don't want to wear the kilt, why don't you play the game in a thong? I'm sure the other team will get a kick out of it."

Suzy blushed and Gator turned to me as she scolded me, "Morgan! You know better than that!" Then she looked at Suzy as she said, "Save the thong for the lingerie practice."

"Lingerie practice?" Suzy repeated, looking horrified.

"The lingerie practice is the one after the practice where we dress up as pirates." Gator replied. It was a joke, but Suzy didn't know that.

"She also has a pink bra with superpowers," I said helpfully. "She flashed it during practice in high school and it made the older girls clinically stupid for a good five minutes."

"Completely understandable," Gator nodded sagely.

"You are lying!" Suzy sputtered, glaring at me. Her face was purple.

I looked at my teammates. "The older girls discussed it at length when we were driving to an away game, and my sister froze it once. It had no effect on me, though. Girls were still icky."

"You grow into it," Fireball shrugged.

"Do you have a thong that matches the super bra?" Gator looked at Suzy. "We don't want you on the pitch looking like a dog from every town."

"You little pervs!" Suzy barked in disgust, stomping off.

CHAPTER 15

Exhibition Condition

The extra practices were hard on all of us, especially me, because I had so much gear to haul. Britany and Liam suggested that until the game was played they would keep my gear bag at their house, and they would bring it to practice in the back of their car. I agreed because I couldn't afford the cost of gas and the daily parking permit if I had to drive to school several times a week. The bag was waiting for me when I got to practice and at the end of practice, I carried it back to their SUV that was always parked behind the field house.

One day Liam was hanging back to talk to the forwards, so it was just me and Britany at the car.

"Can I ask you a psychology question?" I asked as she unlocked the tailgate.

"A psychology question?" Britany repeated, looking at me curiously. "Go ahead."

"What does compartmentalizing mean?" I asked.

I was still thinking about what Gator said weeks earlier.

Britany's eyebrows went up. "Compartmentalizing is when you mentally set something aside — like putting a pan of sauce on the back burner of the stove to simmer when you are cooking with the intent to come back to it later."

"Is it bad?"

Britany shrugged. "It can be, if you don't come back to that pan or whatever it is that you are compartmentalizing. You can't just set things aside and hope they go away."

"But what if you don't want the sauce?" I asked timidly.

Britany gave me a look. "Sometimes, the sauce must be attended to. It has to be stirred or it will boil over."

I shook my head. "I'm not big on sauces." I said. I had been avoiding Suzy. Gator scolded me for it, saying I was avoiding her because I was really trying to avoid the dyke in myself.

Britany laughed, and glanced over her shoulder to make sure we were alone, then she asked in a low voice, "This is about you and Zan, isn't it? And the kilts?" She said Gator told her about the altercation after practice.

"It wasn't a big deal," I said hastily. "I'm trying to stay away from her."

"That may not be a good idea," Britany said reproachfully. She cocked her head to one side as she added, "Morgan, the only people who can hurt us are the people we care about. And obviously, you still care about Zan, and on some level she still cares about you."

"I don't think so," I shook my head. "It bugs me that she treats me like I am still fourteen years old."

"She does talk down to you," Britany agreed, then she let out a snort, adding, "Let's be fair — she talks down to everyone on the team, except for Liam. She is quite opinionated."

"Bootsy says she's dark." I said.

"I agree with that," Britany nodded, growing serious. "It's obvious she's in pain and there is bad blood between you two, and it's being carried on to the pitch. I don't want it getting in the way of the competition."

"Neither do I."

Britany took a deep breath. "Then please do what you can to fix it."

I think it was the idea of messing up the game for the rest of the team that made me finally bite the bullet and approach Suzy. I ran into her on the steps of the library Tuesday morning and asked her to meet me for coffee later that day. She gave me a wary look but agreed.

As we settled down at a back corner table in the student union, both armed with paper cups of the steaming beverage Suzy announced, "I don't want you to get the wrong idea about this. I don't want a relationship with you."

I stared at her. "I don't want a relationship with you either! That's not what this is about."

"Oh!" She looked surprised as she sat back in her chair. "What is this about then?"

"I need some background first. How did you end up at North State?" The question that had been bothering me for weeks. "The last time I saw you, you were trying to get an interview with the aquarium in San Francisco."

Suzy's eyes smoldered.

"A week after I was kicked out of my parent's house I got a letter from the aquarium with a job offer, provided I complete my master's degree." She explained the aquarium had ties to North State and they pulled strings to get her enrolled although classes had already begun. "It was a scramble to get everything into storage and then head north," she continued. She had arrived at NSU two weeks late and she noted, had been behind ever since. "Is that all you wanted to know?" she demanded, glancing at her watch. "Because I really don't have the time–"

"Quit being such a bitch at practice," I cut her off.

Suzy blinked. "What?"

"Everything out of your mouth is an order or a sarcastic comment. It's destroying team morale. You may think you're being helpful, but you're not. Liam is the coach, not you. So stop acting like you're better than the rest of us."

"I was on the Olympic team! I played at one of the most competitive schools in the country! I am better than the rest of the team!" she sputtered incredulously.

"You played on those teams many years ago." I reminded her. "And by better than us, I mean you act like you're a better person than the rest of us, which you're not." I shook my head. "Honestly, I don't remember you being this ugly. What happened?"

Suzy leaned forward, her eyes hard with anger. "I am not going to sit here and let you insult me! I have a lot going on right now and I don't need this!" she snarled. "Field hockey is supposed to be competitive. I had no idea I was playing with a bunch of sugar plums!"

"Sugar plums?" I repeated, wondering if she had taken a good look at Gator and Fireball. "We're not sugar plums. We play for fun. We play for exercise. We play because we like playing together -- except for you. Your constant barrage of negativity is making it really hard for anyone to like you. And yes, I speak for the team." That last part was made up. I was so far out on that limb I heard it cracking behind me. "The rest of us are looking forward to the game against the BC team," I continued. "Please don't ruin this for us."

Suzy's eyes went wide, then she averted her gaze as she asked "Would you like me to quit?" her voice forecast tears.

"No, we need you to have eleven players," I said evenly.

"Wow," Suzy muttered, closing her eyes tight. There was an awkward pause and then a tear slid down her right cheek.

Suddenly I saw my childhood friend sitting across from me looking very vulnerable. I reached out and touched her arm gently. "Hey...what's going on, Wildcat?"

Suzy looked at me. "Hockey is the one fun thing I have right now," she began, and then the floodgates opened. She was taking 18 units to finish her degree by June so she could start the job in July. The classes were harder than she expected and she was starting to doubt she'd be able to finish and do the job she wanted so badly. The aquarium set her up in a shared apartment. She had two roommates who fought constantly, making it very stressful to be home. Winnifred, the love of her life was now attending graduate school in San Francisco and Suzy, excited about the aquarium job, wrote to her suggesting they could finally be together like they used to talk about. Winnifred hadn't replied to Suzy's letters or returned her phone calls and Suzy feared the worst. Then Suzy dropped the bomb: "It wouldn't be so bad if I had my parents to fall back on. When I was an undergrad, I had them to talk to when things got too much. Now I don't," she sobbed. "They disowned me. I'm completely on my own!"

I cringed, knowing I was partially responsible for that. "You're not on your own!" I heard myself say. "I'm here! You can talk to me!"

Suzy was incredulous. "We had a fight, remember? When you didn't say hi to me that first day at practice, I figured you didn't want to be friends anymore."

I squirmed. "I handled that badly," I admitted. "But I didn't know what to say, what to do, or how to act." I sighed. "Can we start over? Can you accept that I am not a kid anymore? I can't do anything about your class load or your roommates, but you can talk to me. And could you please just work on being a little nicer to the team? We're actually a pretty fun group, once you get to know us."

Suzy wiped away her tears with her sleeve. After a few minutes she said "Okay."

"Good," I sighed. "We're The Tomboys of Cherry Lane. We gotta stick together." Suzy laughed and I saluted her with my cup.

News of the exhibition game got around. Britany and Liam were interviewed by the campus media, and the local newspapers and TV stations came out to do stories on us. The university advertised the date and time of the game and moved two extra sets of bleachers to the pitch for more spectators. A few of us started to wonder if maybe Suzy was right, and us playing the British Columbia team was a much bigger deal than we first thought it was.

It was Gator's idea to have the Collective do a program about women in athletics. The gist of the piece was how organized sports had been part of their lives and how they benefited from it. Britany asked her to include Suzy. Britany said Suzy felt isolated from the rest of the team, and that was bad for morale. Gator replied that Suzy had done a good job of isolating herself, but complied with Britany's request.

That Sunday Suzy was late to practice. She showed up halfway through the first drill and out of breath because she had run the two blocks from her apartment. She looked pale and exhausted, so much so that Britany asked her if she was coming down with something. Suzy replied she had just gotten home from San Francisco – by hitch-hiking. She drove down Friday night and the clutch went out on her car on the way back. She'd left her car in a small town halfway between San Francisco and North State. Britany remarked that was risky behavior and Suzy just smirked and shrugged.

During a water break I overheard Suzy telling Bootsy that she'd made the trip to see Winnifred, but it had 'blown up in her face'. I kind of figured that out as she was playing so poorly. She was tackled, missing passes, you name it. Her head wasn't in the game at all.

I felt bad to see her upset. "You look tired," I said gently as I passed her a bottle of Gatorade.

"Thanks a lot," Suzy said defensively. "How do you look when you haven't slept for a week because of your roommates?"

"I don't have roommates," I replied, wondering why she was so hostile. "I live alone."

Suzy stared at me. "How do you afford it?"

"With some difficulty," I admitted.

After practice Gator loaded her truck with the women who agreed to be interviewed and drove us down the hill to the radio station. There were four guests plus Gator on mic, so the room was crowded. Gator did the interviews while I ran the sound board and took notes.

The interviews gave me a chance to learn more about my teammates. Fireball had played semi-professional tennis in high school in addition to field hockey. Shark had been playing since the sixth grade and was on a partial athletic scholarship to NSU because she also ran track in the spring. Britany had been playing since primary school and had a silver and a bronze medal from her time on the Scottish national team. Suzy surprised all of us when she cheerfully opened up, talking about how her older brother encouraged her interest in sports and by middle school they had become her life. Field hockey was the first 'girl' sport she had played. She talked about the athletic scholarships she earned that helped put her through college and led her to being the first alternate on the United States Women's Olympic Field Hockey team. She had particularly fond memories of her college days where the coach worked them so hard that barfing during practice was a regular occurrence.

Monday evening, I was back at the station with Gator editing the piece. We came right from practice, and we smelled like it, but the show must go on. So many voices made the program difficult to edit. We would need the time on Thursday to finish the program.

I was exhausted by the time I got home and in desperate need of a shower and sleep. As I approached the front door I was surprised to see a light on inside my apartment. Had I left one on? There was a note taped to the door: "Don't worry, it's just me. – Suzy".

"Suzy?" I called as I entered.

"In here!" Suzy called sleepily from the bedroom.

She was in bed wearing one of my T-shirts. The reading lamp on the milk crate I used as a nightstand was on, leaving most of the room in darkness. Her backpack was at the foot of the bed with her practice clothes on it.

"What are you doing here?" I asked, hanging my jacket on the back of a kitchen chair.

"I needed sleep," she said, yawning. "My roommates are fighting again. I knew you weren't going to be home for a few hours. I didn't think you'd mind. Your dad gave me your address."

"How did you get in?" I asked, feeling violated on several different levels. "I know I locked the door this morning."

Suzy chuckled, "Your bathroom window was unlocked – I went along the roofline and got in that way."

"What are you wearing?" I blurted out, then cringed at the double-entendre of the remark.

Suzy smiled as she lifted the blanket and looked down at herself, then back up at me. "I borrowed a t-shirt. It was too cold for my Eve in the Garden suit. I didn't think you'd like it if I got into bed in my sweaty practice clothes so I took a shower and grabbed something from the closet. Is that a problem?"

Yes, it was a big problem, I thought, but I replied with a joke, muttering "Is this one of those dreams where I wake up before the good part?"

"No...this is real," Suzy grinned then shivered. "Brrr! It's cold in here! Doesn't your heat work?"

"Only when the people in the house underneath run theirs," I replied sheepishly.

"That sucks," she said, sitting up in bed. "You also need to grocery shop. I checked your fridge. It's pretty much empty."

"I know." I cringed. The only food I had in there was a loaf of bread, PB&J, and a few apples.

"You need a shower," Suzy said, wrinkling her nose.

"I know."

"Do you want some company?" she asked, giving me a teasing look.

"No, I'll be quick," I said, grabbing a clean pair of boxers and a t-shirt that I wore as pajamas and heading into the bathroom. I wondered why I didn't have the guts to tell her to leave, or whether on some level, I wanted her to stay.

Suzy was looking at her watch when I returned. "Three minutes!" she noted. "Some things don't change!"

We looked at each other for a moment in the semi-darkness. "Is there a problem?" she asked.

"I need to get some sleep." I said.

"It works infinitely better if you get in bed first," she said, then yawned, "I could use a few more hours myself. Come on, tuck in."

Reluctantly, I crawled into bed next to her.

"Much better," she said, throwing her arm over me and putting her head on my shoulder. "We need to huddle together for warmth,"

It did feel good to have her next to me, but I could tell there was more to this. "Suzy, what is it you want from me?"

"I want a snuggle and sleep," Suzy said in a childish voice. She had her eyes closed. She put her left hand on my arm, stroking me, then her hand wandered. She definitely wanted more than sleep.

I let out a yelp and jumped out of bed. "That's more than sleep!"

Suzy looked at me like I was crazy. "What is your problem?" she demanded, getting out of bed. I was glad the t-shirt she wore was as long as it was.

"You're making me really uncomfortable," I said, grabbing my bathrobe to cover up.

Suzy giggled. "My, my, you are so easy to embarrass! I'll be on top, just like you wanted!" Then she lunged at me, grabbing me around the waist. She was stronger than she looked, and it surprised me when she threw me on the bed and was on top of me in a flash.

I turned my head when she tried to kiss me. "Suzy, not funny! Please stop!"

Suzy let out a snort. "Enough of the hard-to-get act, Morgan!" she shouted angrily.

I rolled to the right, throwing her off of me then scrambled off the bed. I turned on the overhead light, hoping to destroy the mood.

"Suzy, I don't want to —" I broke off when I got a good look at her. She had a weird gleam in her eyes and her pupils were dilated. I sort of let out a gasp. "Holy crap! Your eyes! What are you on?"

Suzy started to laugh. "Took you long enough!," she said. "Ecstasy. Better than alcohol for losing your inhibitions. You can get it on every street corner in San Francisco."

"Ecstasy?" I repeated. I wasn't sure what that was, but I knew I didn't want any part of it. "This isn't you." I said, backing away from her, shaking my head slowly. It was like someone was wearing a mask of Suzy. "I don't want you here." My words surprised both of us. "Not like this."

She stared at me in disbelief. "What?"

"I want you to leave." She was scaring me.

She glared at me. "Fine,"

She marched over to her clothes and kept her back to me as she started to dress. I stepped into the other room to give her privacy.

A moment later she was dressed and burst through the door. "I don't know what your problem is!" she bellowed.

"I don't want to be with you when you're on something!"

Suzy paused while putting on her sweatshirt. "I had no idea you were this immature," she shook her head.

"Immature?" I sputtered.

"You are such a kid!" Suzy grabbed my letterman jacket from the back of the chair and flung it across the room. "You're twenty-one and still wearing your high school jacket. You're insecure. You think this jacket makes you look cool? It makes you look pathetic!" she spat.

"Goddamn it, Suzy!" I cried as I quickly retrieved my jacket from the floor. "I wear it because it's the only warm jacket I own!"

"You wear it because you're pathetic and stuck in the past," she shouted. "Grow up, Morgan!"

"I am grown up! I'm twenty-one!"

Suzy let out an ugly laugh. "If you were grown up you'd be able to support yourself. You don't have heat, you don't have food -- I bet you're behind on the rent too!"

"Enough with the mouth full of knives!" I snapped, my anger matching her's. "I get it! You're unhappy. And because you're unhappy you have to poison the world around you! If that's who you are now, the world would be a better place without you in it!"

These were horrible, hateful words and they would come back to haunt me.

"It's not me, it's you," she hissed. "If you don't find me attractive, there is something really wrong with you."

"I don't think anyone who needs to be chemically activated to function is attractive," I replied.

"Fuck you, Morgan!"

"No."

Suzy made a noise of disgust and called me every insulting name she could think of or make up then grabbed her backpack and stormed out. I made sure the bathroom window was locked and then I barricaded the front door with the kitchen chairs. I knew I was overreacting, but I didn't care.

CHAPTER 16

Avoid the Dyke, Part Deux

"Wow, you're here early," Gator remarked when she showed up at the radio station on Thursday evening. I was already at work.

"Ground school got out early," I said. I was taking Private Pilot ground school as an elective. The full course spanned three semesters. Because it was mostly reading the FAA textbook it was the one class I didn't have to drop when I left school when Mom died.

We had the last twenty minutes of the interview to get through. When Suzy's voice came on I winced, and Gator noticed.

"What was that? Do you object to what she's saying? Or to her as a person?" Gator asked as I spliced a stumble out of the tape. "She wasn't at practice yesterday, was she?"

"No."

"Is she still bothering you?" Gator gave me a worried glance.

"My place was broken into the other night," I said in a pained voice. I hadn't told anyone about Suzy's unwanted visit.

"Oh! That sucks! What did they get?"

I looked at her as I said miserably, "It wasn't that kind of break-in,"

Gator went pale. "Did someone — were you...hurt?" she gasped, then did a double-take. "Wait a minute — are you telling me Suzy broke into your place?"

I nodded. "She was waiting for me when I got home on Monday night."

"Waiting for you?" Gator repeated. "Waiting for you as in 'waiting' for you? Or...waiting for you?"

"She was in my bed."

Gator let out a snort. "Oh, that is so not subtle!"

"She was on something called ecstasy. Apparently, it makes you very amorous and very strong."

"Oh, not good," Gator shuddered. "That stuff is bad news!"

"What is it?" I asked.

Gator gave me a look like I had dodged a bullet. "It's like a combination of amphetamines and hallucinogens. You make really bad decisions on it. My freshman year roommate used to do it. You lose your inhibitions and get very touchy-feely. It lasts for like eight hours, or more if you binge, and when you come down, you really come down."

"That doesn't sound good," I muttered, wondering why anyone would intentionally want that experience.

"It definitely isn't," Gator agreed. "It is called Tuesday Suicide because most people take it on the weekend, and by Monday, they're coming down and by Tuesday, they are really down. You basically use up a month's worth of serotonin in a few days. I guess that explains why she wasn't at practice yesterday. If she was binging on it she was probably out catting around or sleeping it off."

"She said there is something wrong with me because I don't find her attractive."

Gator made a face. "What an ego!" Then she gave me a look. "Did you consent anyway?"

"Good God, no!" I cried, recoiling. "I am never doing that again!"

Gator looked surprised. "Wait – did you just say that you never want to have sex again? Are you sure about that?"

"I don't want it to be chemically activated," I said quickly. "The next time I have physical relations, I don't want to be drunk or on something, I don't want her to be drunk or on something. I want us to be together because we care about each other, not because we're chemically compromised or upset about something,"

"Wow," Gator looked at me in amazement, her face softening. "That's very sweet, Morgan."

"So there's nothing wrong with me? Twice she had to be on something to be with me. Am I that bad?" I asked, my voice trembling.

"No! Of course not!" Gator cried, shaking her head. "Her having to be on something says something about her, not about you," she said, rubbing my back in a sisterly fashion as she continued, "There's nothing wrong with you, Morgan, you're just a romantic." Then she took a deep breath adding, "And someday, you'll find someone who feels the same way you do, and you'll have a wonderful relationship."

"I hope it's not soon," I sighed. "I don't think I'm mature enough for a relationship,"

Gator smiled at me. "You may surprise yourself," she said.

That night I came home to a note on my door from Suzy. She said she was sorry I had become so upset by her uninvited visit. She wrote she didn't have time for games, and suggested I grow up before I went looking for a relationship.

When I told Gator about the note, I learned a new phrase: passive-aggressive. Gator summed it up by saying, "It's not really an apology. She's refusing to take responsibility for her actions by blaming you for being uncomfortable."

"So she's not sorry?" I translated.

"No, she's not." Gator shook her head. "Whatever you do, do not respond to her. Be cool to her at practice, avoid her on campus. Remember, if you don't feed a stray dog it goes away."

"Got it." I said.

CHAPTER 17

Playing the Game

The team from British Columbia arrived in town on Wednesday morning and joined us on the pitch that afternoon for a scrimmage. They wore practice uniforms consisting of red t-shirts and blue kilts with red socks. They all looked lean and fit as they moved onto the pitch single file. We were all in black, per Britany's instructions, and compared to the women from BC, we looked like a bunch of theater arts majors. I can't speak for the rest of my team, but I was intimidated. It seemed like the whole BC team was at least six inches taller than me — the goalie was the same size as Gator and when she stood before me in her red goalie kit, I felt like I should hurry back to Lilliput to help tie down Gulliver.

The BC team brought two referees with them. That freed up Liam to be on the sidelines capturing the action with a video camera. After practice we went over to Liam and Britany's house to watch the video to look for trends and weaknesses that we could exploit. They lived just off campus on the other side of the freeway accessible by the pedestrian bridge. Some NSU students referred to the bridge as "Losers Leap" because years ago an NSU student went through the chain-link fencing and killed himself by jumping onto the freeway below. Earlier that year someone had cut a hole in the chain-link with the intent of jumping, but didn't finish the job. The hole was maybe a foot and a half wide, and the would-be jumper got stuck in the fence. The city had put yellow caution tape across the hole but hadn't fixed it yet. The bridge gave me the creeps, so I walked across it quickly.

Britany directed us into their basement recreation room. The room was lined with trophy cases and every award was for field hockey. In the center of the room was a pool table. Against the far wall was a jukebox filled with rock and roll records from the 1950s and early 1960s. One wall was dominated by a big television and a VCR set up. There were several benches in front of it. Britany passed out bottles of water, pencils and pieces of notebook paper — telling us all to take notes as Liam used the video of the scrimmage to give us an illustrated lecture on the strategy we should use against the BC team. We had lost the scrimmage 4 to 1. I winced when the video of the other team scoring came up on screen. Gator, sitting next to me, patted me on the shoulder comfortingly, reminding me that we were a team, so when the opposition scored it was because they had gotten through several lines of defense before reaching me — and we couldn't win unless our offense scored, and it was all part of the game.

During the lecture I glanced over at Suzy. It had been a week since her surprise visit and thus far I managed to avoid her. She seemed to be avoiding me too. She was nervously twisting the grip on her stick as she watched the video and I wondered if she was coming down from a binge.

We'd worked so hard a a team it was a relief when game day finally arrived. Now we'd show what we were made of, standing tall before the Canadians. At least that's what Britany told us. I was anxious, as it had been years since I played in a real game, and because Saturday would be the first time I would be in a women's locker room since I figured out I was gay. I was worried it was going to be weird. I told Gator I couldn't imagine looking at the other women, but wasn't sure what I should do. Gator, who claimed to have known she was gay since high school smiled and patted my arm as she said briskly, "Eyes down! Count the tiles on the floor when heading in and out of the shower, keep your eyes on your locker, get in, get dressed, get out."

"What if I accidentally see a pink bra?" I asked. "Will it affect me now?"

Gator frowned and shook her head. "The pink bra, while powerful, is not everyone's Kryptonite. Plus pretty much everyone wears black sports bras and those are hardly sexy."

There was a lot of ritual involved in the game. It started by dressing up to report to the locker room. Britany told us to dress in any manner that gave us confidence, saying many of the women on the teams she had played on wore suits like they were going to a job interview. The only suit I had was the one I wore to funerals and didn't want to wear that, so I decided on black jeans, my gold sweatshirt and gold laces in my white Nike high tops. Over this, I wore my letterman jacket. Gator, dressed in khakis and a sweater called my outfit a "jock girl power suit" when she picked me up that afternoon.

We dressed out quickly and right on time we filed into the team room where Britany, dressed in her uniform with the captain's armband, was waiting for us, waving her stick like it was Excalibur.

"Come in! Come in, ladies, come in!" She gestured for us to sit down on the benches. She paced back and forth, twirling her field hockey stick in her right hand like a baton. "Today is the big day! Are we excited and ready to play?"

The team sort of laughed and looked puzzled, then it occurred to me what she wanted – Coach Norton used to do the same thing to get us pumped before games. I looked across the room at Suzy – her eyes flickered with the same sense of recognition that I felt, so I nodded at her and we both replied, "Yes, ma'am!"

Britany laughed and nodded, pointing at me then at Suzy. "That's the spirit!" Then she put her hand up to her ear as she repeated, "Are we excited and ready to play?"

"YES, MA'AM!" the team bellowed.

Britany twirled her stick one more time as she asked, "Does everyone have their mouthguard and shin guards?"

"YES, MA'AM!"

Britany nodded Land then started to tap her stick slowly on the floor, rhythmically playing quarter notes as she gave us instructions for the game. (Tap, tap, tap, tap) "Okay ladies, there are just eleven of us, so we all play the full game. (Tap, tap, tap, tap) Let's remember the protocol: Spot, Octi, Beverly, and Parrot! Feed the forwards, protect the back field! (Tap, tap, tap, tap) Fireball, Bootsy, Shark, and Zan! Keep the ball moving forward! (Tap, tap, tap, tap) Zan! On corners, you will fly! Beverly! Protect Gator! Gator, protect Wolf! (Tap, tap, tap, tap) And Wolf-" she narrowed her eyes at me. "You protect that goal like your babies are in there! And no growling!"

"Yes, ma'am!" I shouted in a volume and register that would have made my Marine Corps father proud.

The team laughed and Britany cried out "Join me ladies!" We all started to tap our sticks on the cement floor in unison. "Repeat after me... We are the NSU field hockey team!"

"WE ARE THE NSU FIELD HOCKEY TEAM!"

"We will do our best on the pitch!"

"WE WILL DO OUR BEST ON THE PITCH!"

"We will have fun and be good sports!"

"WE WILL HAVE FUN AND BE GOOD SPORTS!"

Then Britany lifted her stick over her head, pointing to the door as she cried, "Let's go!" We filed out behind her, marching single file to the ramp that led to the pitch. I swear we were in step.

"Holy frog legs!" I gasped when we reached the top.

There were three sets of bleachers set up on the sidelines — and they were all filled with people dressed in green and gold. They cheered when they saw us. There was a sound system and an announcer.

"And here they come, the North State Women's Field Hockey team!" he yelled dramatically and the crowd let out a roar. The Marching Lumberjacks, the North State marching band, was also at the top of the ramp. They launched into the school fight song when they saw us.

Britany let out a bark of laughter then broke into a trot, leading us to our bench on the side of the pitch as the crowd, bundled up because it was damp and a little chilly, leapt to their feet singing the North State Fight Song along with the band. Some of the folks had old-style North State pennants that they waved in time to the music. Others had hand-lettered signs that read NORTH STATE FIELD HOCKEY RULES! and WE LOVE NS FH!

As we shed our warmup jackets the announcer talked about the North State team being a club and how this game was a big deal for us since the school had cut the field hockey program several years earlier. He told the crowd we were a club team facing a nationally ranked team from British Columbia.

Oh God, I thought to myself as I headed to the west goal to warm up. A squadron of bats — not butterflies, bats — settled in my stomach. My team joined me and balls zipped back and forth inside the shooting circle for shots on goal and practice passes.

Suddenly E*ye of the Tiger* from *Rocky III* blared across the field as the BC team, in red and white kit stormed the field, lining up on the opposite sideline. One of their support staff had carried a boombox. Their team captain stood before them and led them in synchronized warm up. They advanced instep to the music like a drill team.

My team shared a look. I think we were intimidated, with the exception of Britany who rolled her eyes, and then shouted at the BC team "Oh calm down!"

Both teams lined up for the presentation of the colors. We faced the flagpole and stood at attention as the marching band played *The Star Spangled Banner*. It was a special kind of thrill to be representing both my school and my country as I stood singing with my helmet under my arm and my hand over my heart. Then we stood at attention as the band launched into *O Canada* and the BC flag was raised on a second flagpole. The players from BC stood with their arms linked as they sang their national anthem.

The two-minute warning horn sounded. We won the coin toss and Britany announced we would defend the west goal first. We then huddled at the midfield and Britany led us in a cheer of "GO! SCORE! WIN! NORTH STATE!" and we took our positions.

I faced the pitch as I shuffled left, then right, tapping each freshly painted goal post. It was my way of getting my bearings. The tournament bats were flying loops in my stomach.

An airhorn announced the start of the game. We were playing tournament rules, so the game consisted of two twenty-five minute halves with a five-minute halftime. We played a 4-4-2-1 formation, that is, four forwards made up of two inside and two wings, four midfielders, two defenders, and me in the goal. I had never played in a tournament before so this was all new to me.

The BC team took possession quickly. As the forwards came toward me I was acutely aware these were a national team, not high school girls. Gator, Beverly and Parrot did their best to defend, but the BC team made it into the circle. I was able to block the shot that came, but the BC forward, a woman with legs as tall as I was, slammed into me and we both went down. I guess

I growled at her, because as we untangled ourselves to a chorus of whistles, one of the BC referees gave me a sharp look as she demanded, "Were you growling?"

"It wasn't a growl, that was German," said Gator who was a few feet behind me during the tackle. She quickly threw me a look. "She was speaking in her native tongue. She's German. Isn't that right, Wolfie?"

"Yah!" I nodded, in my best German accent learned from watching *Hogan's Heroes* reruns as a kid.

The referee called for a short corner, which was the normal call after a penalty in the defense circle. Most goals came from short corners — and every field hockey player knows it. The offense lines up at the top of the circle, ready to swarm the cage like sharks going after blood in the water. The defense lines up in the goal cage and along the back line. At the whistle the selected offensive player hits the ball from the corner to a player at the top of the circle who then tries to score. The defensive players can't move until the ball is hit, and the defense must sprint to try to stop the offense from getting a shot off. The tension was starting to rise like humidity on a summer day.

As we moved into position, I gave Gator a sidelong look.

"German?"

"Only thing I could think of," Gator shrugged.

Suddenly Suzy was next to me, looking angry. She grabbed my arm and hissed in my ear "Red card!" It was a warning.

Gator was on the other side of me. She reached over and pushed Suzy away. "Back off!" Gator's eyes snapped with anger.

Suzy looked startled, but then she moved down to my right, back to being focused on the game. Gator got into position on my left. Without looking at her I whimpered "I love you, Gator."

"I know," Gator shrugged.

The whistle blew. The shot went across the zone to the waiting attacker who drilled it toward the goal. I blocked it with my mitt then booted it to the left side of the pitch where Parrot intercepted it, passing it up field to Beverly who in turn fed it to Shark, who easily outran the BC player trying to guard her. Shark drove the ball across the pitch to Suzy, who whirled and took a shot on goal, driving it hard and high, just like the old days.

"North State scores!" the announcer crowed. The crowd roared and the marching band launched into the school fight song again, just like they did at football games when the team scored. My teammates jogged back to the starting position, celebrating with fist pumps and stick taps.

Gator looked over her shoulder at me and grinned "There's one for safety!" meaning we now had one on the scoreboard.

Getting scored on lit a fire under the BC team. At the whistle they came toward the goal fast and fierce, breaking past our midfield and even Gator, who collided with a player during a tackle sending them both down on the pitch.

"Out of the cage! Out of the cage!" Gator yelled, scrambling to her feet as two BC players descended on me.

I charged the attacker with the ball, cutting down her angle to the cage. She rushed the shot which I easily blocked and cleared to the side. The crowd cheered. My heart was pounding as I scrambled back to position. I was relieved when Beverly scooped up the ball and sent it up the pitch where Suzy and Britany were waiting.

The action seesawed back and forth. It was the most physical game I had ever played, and the fastest. In the first half there were multiple pile ups in the goal cages — three in mine, two in the BC cage, and all came as a result of short corners. During one, a BC player blocked me by backing into me. I scrambled to get around her, but I wasn't fast enough before she passed the ball to a teammate who took the shot. I lunged but missed. I spun around to see Gator, crouching down holding her stick parallel to the ground. The ball went right past Gator in the tiny gap between her and the post. As a shrill whistle announced the goal, Gator looked at me. There was disappointment in her eyes as she said "I'm sorry Wolf, that one was on me," She looked ready to cry.

"It got through all of us!" I reminded her.

The action continued. There were several shots on both goals by both teams. The crowd roared every time we took a shot or I stopped one. Toward the end of the first half the BC players reached the top of the defense circle and my team was there to stop them. There was a pile up and Shark and two BC players went down in a clatter of sticks. Shark let out a scream of pain just as the air horn announced the end of the first half.

Gator and Fireball helped carry a grimacing Shark to the sidelines where bags of ice were applied to her left knee, which was swelling and turning an angry purple. Shark wouldn't be able to finish the game and we didn't have any substitute players.

Britany looked at us as we huddled around our injured teammate. "We can forfeit, or we can keep playing with ten players," she said, answering the question we all had before we even asked it.

"Play!" we all said.

Liam quickly pulled out his magnetic coach board to explain how we would have to adjust our strategy to make up for our reduced numbers. "Don't be like seven-year-olds playing soccer," Liam warned us. "Don't be in such a hurry to pass. Make the pass count!"

As we took the field for the second half the announcer explained we had lost a player due to injury, so we were now outnumbered. That didn't mean the BC team went any easier on us. There were more attempts on goal which I blocked. In the second half I stopped nine attempts on goal and my adrenalin was surging and I gloried in it. I didn't remember field hockey being this emotionally satisfying when I was a kid and I wanted that feeling to last forever.

The game was tied one to one when the horn signaled the end of the match. I was surprised to learn that tournament rules called for a penalty shootout competition to determine the winner. Penalty shootouts require the goalkeeper to stand with their heels on the goal line while the attacker is in the center of the circle approximately seven yards in front of them with the ball on the ground. When the referee blows the whistle, the attacker takes the shot. It's just the goalkeeper facing an attacker. It's intense. I had never done it before in a real game, all I could think about was letting my team down, and I was in a panic.

"Wolf, you are our goalie!" Fireball said encouragingly, as she saw the fear in my eyes.

"Make yourself big in the goal! Focus! You got this!" Gator urged.

"North State, you're up first," said the referee, nodding at me.

I took my position and found myself facing off against a dark-haired woman that I suspected (rightfully so) was the best player from the BC team.

"Player ready?" The referee looked at my opponent. She nodded. "Keeper ready?" he looked at me. I nodded. The whistle sounded and a fast low shot went into the cage to my left. The BC team cheered. The crowd groaned and my team shouted encouragement.

I quickly stepped out to allow the BC goalie to take the cage. She was up against Fireball, who on the whistle, quickly and neatly slammed one low and to the right. The crowd went wild. The score was now tied.

I stepped back into the cage and concentrated on staying on my toes. This time, instead of looking at the player, I just looked at the ball. When the whistle sounded the ball was struck and I lunged to the right. The shot bounced off the goal post and then me — but didn't go in. It is hard to say who was cheering more — the people in the bleachers or my team.

Suzy was the next attacker for our side. She easily set one high and to the right to score. The North State fans roared in approval and the announcer told the crowd this next attempt could determine the outcome of the game.

A hush fell over the pitch as I stepped into the cage. I positioned myself on the line and held my arms up high.

"Player ready? Keeper ready?"

The whistle blew. The shot was low to the left. I lunged and it hit the leg guard and bounced up at eye level. I slapped it down with my mitt — no goal — and a long shrill whistle blast announced the end of the game. North State had won! The band launched into the fight song as my team surrounded me shouting "WOLF! WOLF! WOLF! WOLF!" as they patted me on the back and on the head. I howled in triumph and my team answered me — even Suzy.

The crowd was on their feet cheering us as we gave the traditional cheer thanking the other team and the officials, then filed past the BC team single file, tapping their sticks and thanking them for the game. Then Liam called us into a huddle, praising us for our performance, saying he had never seen such heart in a competition and that we had 'left it all on the pitch'. He looked very pleased as he said "We have won the game, and now we will win the party," he looked at Britany who smirked and nodded.

"Get showered, get changed and we'll see you at the house," she grinned.

CHAPTER 18

Over the Rainbow

A caravan of cars with freshly showered field hockey players headed over to Liam and Britany's. Two carloads of pizza were ordered, and a keg of beer was set up on the back deck next to several ice chests filled with soda and bottled water. The keg was tapped quickly. I grabbed a Dr. Pepper right off the bat as I was determined to stay sober.

It was a tradition that the teams serenaded each other after a match. We were at the jukebox taking turns singing along with the oldies, and there was dancing. When the Dupree's *Somewhere Over the Rainbow* started to play Suzy, slightly drunk and happy because she had scored two goals, pulled me onto the dance floor, saying this was 'our song'. I had never danced with a woman before.

"Which one of us leads?" I asked.

"You do, you play defense," she said.

"Okay," I put my hand on her hip.

As I twirled her on the dance floor she sighed dramatically, "Morgan, where the hell were you when I was twenty?"

"In high school." I replied.

Suzy roared with laughter. She asked if we could put the past behind us and be friends again. Between the post-game endorphins and the music, my guard was down and I said "yes." to both.

The BC women really liked their adult beverages, especially the hard stuff — they had brought several bottles of rum and whiskey with them. The latter was consumed neat, while the rum was folded into daiquiris made by Britany and Shark utilizing two blenders in the kitchen. The BC team was drinking us under the table.

I was shooting pool with some of the BC midfielders when Britany came downstairs holding a big pot and a lid.

"Wolfie! Are you sober?" she asked. It was obvious she wasn't.

"Yes, ma'am!" I replied.

Britany held the pot and lid out to me. "Then I designate you our official popcorn maker. The rest of us are a bit tipsy and probably shouldn't be near the stove,"

"People are hungry? After all that pizza?" I asked incredulously.

"Apparently, yes!" Then Britany drew herself up tall and asked, quite seriously, with her accent sharp as it could be, "Wolfie, can you serve your team?"

I handed my pool cue to the woman next to me, came to attention and saluted Britany as I replied crisply, "Yes, ma'am! Right away ma'am!" I took the pot and the lid and quickly marched upstairs.

I was slaving over the stove when Gator, up from the rec room, told me that Suzy had made a friend on the BC team. They were in a dark corner of the basement, very drunk and making out like a couple of freshmen.

"Good for her!" I snorted, trying to ignore the twinge in my gut. I reminded myself she had to be drunk to have a relationship and I didn't want to go down that road again.

"Does anyone object to butter on the popcorn?" Britany yelled above the sound of the party. An unintelligible roar was the reply and she handed me a stick of butter saying, "Have at it!"

I made three batches of popcorn in short order. We ran out of bowls, so Britany was dumping the popcorn into coffee mugs, cake pans, anything to feed the women who gobbled it up like they were starving.

"Why is everyone so hungry?" I mused as I started on the fourth batch.

"I think the ladies are ovulating?" Britany suggested, handing me another stick of butter. "Ovulation combined with a college-level match makes you want to eat everything in sight."

"Yes, ma'am, of course, ma'am," I said, turning back to the stove.

Suddenly there was a scream behind me. "WOOOOOOOOOOOOOLLLLLLLLLLFFFF! I NEED WOOOOOOLLLLLLF! WHO IS WOLF?"

I turned around to see one of the BC forwards tumble into the kitchen. Her clothes were wet and she was crying.

"I'm Wolf," I said, alarmed. "What's going on?"

"Wolf, you need to come now," she gasped, grabbing my arm.

"Zan is on the bridge and wants to jump! Bootsy's out there now! She said you need to come now!"

I dropped the pan and sprinted out of the house. As I approached the bridge deck, I saw Bootsy standing next to the hole in the fence. If I live to be a hundred years old, I will never forget the look of fear on Bootsy's face. Suzy was on the other side of the fence a few feet from the hole. She was standing on the narrow ledge with her back to the bridge holding on to the fence with both hands. Her blouse was torn and hanging in shreds. She was staring straight ahead as a cold rain fell.

"Suzy! Get back in here!" I shouted, sounding a lot harsher than I meant too. Suzy shook her head wordlessly as tears went down her face.

"She's frozen," Bootsy said in a low voice.

Okay, if that's the way you want to play this, I thought, and at that moment I ate the whole bowl of stupid. I knew my sweatshirt was too bulky to fit through the hole, so I peeled it off and started through the hole in my jeans and t-shirt. I felt metal grab my t-shirt and tear my shoulder as I moved out onto the ledge.

Bootsy screamed, lunging for me. I let out a roar that made her stop cold. Gator, who had just arrived, had no such reservation as she reached through the hole and grabbed my wrist. I bit her without even thinking about it. She let go and stepped back, swearing blue and green. She was joined by Fireball and Liam, both breathing hard from the sprint, who glared at me, angry and helpless– I don't know if they were too scared, too large or too smart to go out on the ledge.

I clutched the fence and faced the bridge, inching my way to Suzy as more members of both teams were arriving letting out exclamations of concern and surprise.

The cold made my fingers go numb. "Come back inside, Suzy!" I said evenly, trying not to think about the fact we were on a narrow ledge 60 feet over a highway. Cars were whizzing by below us and we were both shivering.

"Jokes' over, we need to get back on the other side of the fence," I said in a shaky voice.

"No," Suzy warbled. "I'm making the world a better place."

I recognized my words, and it was like getting a punch in the gut.

"Please come back inside the fence," I begged. I was still two feet away from her.

Suzy shook her head wordlessly.

On the other side of the fence Britany made a sort of noise with her mouth to get my attention. She made eye contact with me and mouthed the words "keep talking".

I nodded slightly then looked at Suzy as I said gently, "We're going back inside, okay?"

"No!" Suzy screamed so loudly I flinched. She looked at me, hyperventilating as she said "I can't do this anymore," she cried. She looked terrified.

"You can do anything," I heard myself say. "You are Suzanne Marie Mathews. You're the older sister of Butchie and the younger sister of Rickie. You taught me to ride a bicycle, catch a frog, throw a football, throw a punch, shoot marbles, climb trees, play field hockey, and make waffles. You were on the Olympic

Field Hockey team. You put the 'wild' in Wildcat and we all look up to you. We don't want to lose you."

Suzy shook her head and let out a cry like a wounded animal.

I responded with the Wildcat growl as I reached her and put my arm across her body protectively. "You're okay," I whispered. "I'm the goalie, my job is to protect you."

Suzy looked at me, and her eyes went wide, as if she suddenly realized where she was. "I'm scared," she whispered.

So am I, I thought, then I started to sing *"Somewhere over the rainbow...way up high..."*

She looked at me in surprise, but it seemed to reach her, so I sang the second line *"There's a land that I heard of..."*

"Once in a lullaby," came a voice from the other side of the fence then the rest of the women and Liam started to sing. They continued to sing as I grabbed hold of Suzy's blouse then her waist and dragged her to the hole. Multiple hands reached for us and we tumbled onto the bridge. I wrapped my arms and legs around her. She grabbed my arms and sobbed hysterically, telling me how sorry she was. We were both shaking and I was growling protectively.

"Calm down, Wolfie!" Britany cried, dropping to her knees in front of me. "The danger has passed! You are both safe!"

"Here," Fireball handed me my sweatshirt which I pulled over Suzy's head. She was so cold her teeth were chattering in the remnants of her blouse and pink bra.

The sound of a siren in the distance got everyone's attention.

"We need to get out of here," Liam said urgently. He looked at Britany. "We can't be caught here." Since they were both professors and had thrown the party, they were technically responsible for the behavior of the guests.

Britany nodded to Fireball who picked up Suzy in a fireman's carry as if she weighed nothing as Liam shouted "Visiting players, North State women! Back to the house!" and we took off running.

Britany instructed us to put Suzy in the guest bedroom. It was tiny, barely large enough for the twin-sized bed pushed up against the wall. A star-shaped night-light provided the only illumination when we entered.

"Keep the lights off," Britany ordered in a hushed voice. She ducked out, returning a moment later with a bath towel and a large t-shirt. "Dry her off and put her in this," she tossed the shirt to Gator.

Suzy cried softly as we tended to her. Britany very maternally tucked Suzy in while Fireball and Gator hung Suzy's wet clothes over the radiator so they would dry.

"Morgan?" Suzy cried weakly.

"I'm here," I said, taking a seat on the edge of the bed.

"Are you mad at me?" she whimpered.

Before I could answer Britany touched my arm and shook her head. "Of course not," I said quickly.

"You said the world would be a better place if I wasn't in it! Do you really hate me that much, Morgan?" she sobbed.

Britany, Gator, and Fireball gasped. I could feel their eyes on me as I replied, "Not at all." I started to cry. "We were both angry. We both said things we didn't mean," *At least I hoped we did*, I thought.

"Zan, none of us want you to die," Britany said in her therapist voice. "Get some sleep now. things will be better in the morning." She looked at Gator and Fireball. "You two take the first watch."

"Certainly," said Fireball, taking position across the foot of the bed while Gator stretched out on the carpet like an oversized cat.

Britany dragged me into the bathroom. She sat me down on the edge of the tub as she said angrily, "You are injured, and you look like a drowned rat." She dropped a towel over my head and gestured to my shoulder where there was a large bloody scrape that was freely bleeding in the warmth of the house. My t-shirt was also ripped, and the red blood showed up dramatically on the white.

"Oh boy," I was suddenly very glad I was sitting down.

Britany gave me a funny look. "Don't tell me you faint at the sight of blood?"

"Okay, I won't," I said, cringing.

As she pressed a towel against the cut to stop the bleeding Britany told me how stupid I was for going out on the ledge like that, and demanded to know what the hell I was thinking? I shrank in fear and shame as I told her about the fight we'd had.

"It was my fault she was out there," I said, my voice breaking, "I don't know why I said something so terrible."

"You said it because she hurt you and you wanted to hurt her," she shook her head. "This wasn't just hurt feelings and alcohol, was it? What is she on?"

"Ecstasy," I said.

Britany's eyes bulged. "Did you know she used it? Why didn't you say something when she joined the team?" she demanded.

"I just found out the other night!" I yelped. "She showed up in — " I almost said, 'my bed' but caught myself, amending it to "my apartment unannounced."

"You could have said something! She is coming down hard!"

Britany scowled.

"I didn't know she was coming down! I thought she was just drunk!" I cried. I started to tremble violently as I added, "If she had jumped, it would have been all my fault!"

"Rubbish! If she had jumped, it wouldn't have been your fault, but you would have blamed yourself," Britany scolded me, then looked thoughtful, and started to smile. "How did you think of singing *Somewhere Over the Rainbow?* That was brilliant!"

"It's her favorite movie," I said. "The only thing Suzy ever admitted to being afraid of when she was a kid was the Wicked Witch in *The Wizard of Oz*. I figured it would remind her that she could overcome her fears."

"Well done," Britany nodded.

Pretty much everyone spent the night. I wound up in the living room in a pile of blankets and other players flopped together like puppies. I would have slept on the floor of the guest room to be near Suzy, but there wasn't room with Gator and Fireball in there.

Fireball and Suzy were the first up the next morning. Suzy was puzzled to find herself in just her thong and a t-shirt that wasn't hers. She claimed not to remember the night's activities beyond dancing in the basement. Fireball, while giving Suzy a ride home, gave her the details. Suzy burst into tears when she learned of the scene she had made. She was wearing my sweatshirt because her blouse was shredded by the fence.

The team stood down for two weeks because of midterms,

and I continued to stay away because I was embarrassed and ashamed. I felt responsible for Suzy's behavior. Gator, who was still attending practice told me half the team had been knocked for a loop by what she called 'The Suzy Vortex'. As a result, Britany had been setting up counseling sessions for people at the school health center.

I had been away from practice for the better part of a month when I ran into Bootsy in the library. I greeted her awkwardly and Bootsy blurted out "Suzy's gone."

I thought she meant Suzy was dead. I collapsed on to a bench, and through tears I asked how she did it. Bootsy quickly amended her statement, saying Suzy had dropped out of school. She was no longer in class or her apartment. Then Bootsy broke down and tearfully told me she felt responsible for the scene on the bridge. A few days before the game as they walked home together Suzy said she was devastated over losing Winnifred and was feeling self-destructive. Bootsy, not knowing Suzy very well, thought she meant she was going to have rebound sex, so she wasn't surprised when a drunk Suzy announced she was taking the BC player home to bed. Bootsy was ready to call it a night, and as the three of them were walking together Suzy suddenly bolted for the hole in the fence.

Truth be told, I already had a feeling Suzy was gone. Two days after the party I came home and found my sweatshirt on the stoop. There was no note. The shirt smelled like Suzy. I knew I wouldn't ever be able to wear it again, so I threw it away. I didn't reach out to her because I didn't know what to say. Eventually, I rejoined the team, and no one ever mentioned Suzy again. She had become a bad dream we all wanted to forget.

CHAPTER 19

Babies and Paint

"Make sure the paint is lead-free," Dad cautioned as we meandered through the aisles of the hardware store. "The little ones tend to chew."

"I think everything is lead-free now, Dad," I remarked, grabbing a gallon can labeled Sage Green. "Not like when I was a kid."

Dad looked at me, a teasing gleam in his eye. "As I recall you were the one that chewed on everything, my little wolf child,"

"Of course, Dad." I said, pausing to zip up my leather jacket because it was cold in the store.

Dad grabbed a plastic shopping basket and started to pick out brushes and other supplies as he mused "I still cannot believe your sister is having twins. Your mother would be so proud!"

"I'm sure," I said quietly. It had been six years since Mom's passing. I was out of college and employed as a television reporter. I had earned my commercial pilot certificate, and last week I had been accepted to Air Force Officer's Candidate School and would report for training in a month. Laura's twins were due in a week but the nursery wasn't quite ready because five-year-old John had fallen out of a tree and broken his leg. Taking care of him had derailed the preparations for the twins. Dad stepped in to help and drafted me to assist. He was happy that he had more grand-children on the way. He had missed out on Laura's first pregnancy because she was angry with him for dating after Mom died. They made up when she found out she was carrying twins.

"Do you know who owns this store?" Dad asked. "The Mathews family. Do you remember them? They used to live across the street from us and you went to high school with them. Suzy Mathews was part of your rat pack, I think."

"Rat pack?" I repeated. I hadn't seen Suzy since that night on the overpass and hearing her name made my blood go cold.

"Didn't she go to college with you?"

"Briefly," I said, a shiver going through me. I didn't like to think about Suzy. It had been really hard to see someone I revered so much when I was growing up fall apart like that. It was almost a relief when she dropped out of school and out of my life with no goodbye. "Shouldn't Mr. Mathews be retired by now?" I asked, hoping I wouldn't see him. I wonder if he was still angry with me for bedding his daughter.

"The store is a hobby," Dad said. "He needed something to keep him busy after Celia died."

Celia was Mrs. Mathews.

"I'm glad he found something," I said automatically. I had a vague memory of Dad telling me when Mrs. Mathews died from cancer a few years back. At the time, I thought about sending a card of condolence to Suzy but decided it was too weird. Besides, I didn't know where to send it.

"I really think he did this to give Butch a job," Dad muttered. Butch Mathews had been in and out of scrapes with the law since he was a teenager, but, according to Dad, he had pulled himself together. Suzy, he heard, was practicing environmental law in San Francisco. I was surprised, since she wanted to work at the aquarium. Dad concluded by saying that after Mom died and he stopped going to the Gourmet Group he had pretty much lost contact with the Mathews family. "I think they were more your mother's friends," he said.

I agreed with him, since the alternative would have been to tell him about the day Mr. and Mrs. Mathews caught me in bed with Suzy. Dad knew I was gay though. I came out to him after college. He said he didn't care as long as I was happy.

As we approached the cash register Dad remarked, "I think that's Butch?"

I looked. The young man behind the counter was about six feet tall and slightly overweight with dark hair and eyes. I peered at him, trying to see the angry sixteen-year-old I remembered him as. He was in his late twenties now.

Dad used cash to pay for the paint and other supplies. "Please say hello to your father and sister for us," he said, pocketing the receipt.

Butch paused and stared at us. "Wait a minute... I know you!"

Dad grinned and held out his hand.

"Robert Flynn. Do you remember my daughter Morgan?"

Butch grinned. "Hi! So nice to see you!" Dad's hand got a shaking and as he was shaking mine Butch said, "Hey! Dad has the day off, but Suzy is in the back if you want to say hi?"

A wave of relief went over me because Mr. Mathews wasn't there, quickly followed by a wave of panic because Suzy was there. Then it occurred to me that if Suzy was working in the family business she must have made up with her father, but that didn't mean she would want to see me.

"Oh, we don't want to bother her," I said, my pulse pounding in my ears, but Butch was already calling the stockroom.

A moment later Suzy, in jeans and a gray sweatshirt with a paint-stained shop apron appeared, wiping her hands on a rag. Her hair was longer now, cut in sort of a pageboy style. She was pale, and the lines around her eyes and mouth made her look older than her early thirties. She was still thin, but not as thin as she had been in college.

Butch grinned as he gestured to me and Dad. "Recognize these two? You remember Mr. Flynn and Morgan, don't you?"

Suzy blinked. "Oh! Hi! What brings you in today?" She was looking at Dad more than me.

"We're getting paint for the nursery. The family is about to be blessed with twins," Dad said proudly.

Suzy's eyes went wide and she switched her gaze to me. "You're expecting twins?" she sputtered, looking me up and down. "You don't look pregnant!"

"Really? Because I'm due next week," I replied with a straight face. "No, it's not me, it's Laura,"

"Morgan here is a pilot and TV reporter." Dad threw his arm around me. "She's heading into the Air Force soon."

"I guess that explains the flight jacket," Suzy chuckled, looking as uncomfortable as I felt.

"How long have you been working in the family business?" Dad asked. "I thought you were practicing law?"

Butch got a perplexed look on his face and Suzy stiffened as she explained she was helping out so her dad could have a day off. Then she gestured over her shoulder. "I have to get back to work. I'm mixing up a big order in the back. Nice to see you again." She nodded and left as quickly as she had appeared.

Dad didn't say anything until we got to the car. "Was that awkward? Did you two have a falling out?"

"I think she was just busy," I lied, looking at the parking lot so he wouldn't see my eyes misting. I never told Dad about that night on the overpass -- I never talked about it with anyone. And I was going to keep it that way.

CHAPTER 20

Goodbye, Dad

"*S*orry for your loss,"

I had been hearing that phrase so much I was starting to wish that I had a flask to play 'Sorry for Your Loss the Drinking Game'. It was a bright spring day and I was in the cemetery standing next to my parents' graves. Three months earlier Dad had been diagnosed with lung cancer. Last week he finally lost the battle. Dad said it was his own fault he got cancer because he had been a smoker during his eight years in the Marines. He quit cold turkey when Mom got pregnant with Laura, but apparently the damage was done. It was hard to see him go from a sturdy, athletic man who routinely bicycled five miles a day to a stooped old man who got winded walking to the bathroom. I was glad he was out of pain.

With Dad's death I had a strange sense of turning a corner. I was in my forties and, I felt, officially and finally an adult. I had a few stumbles on the way. The military career was cut short by down-sizing, and I didn't have the experience to be an airline pilot nor did I want to be a glorified bus driver, so I found a job as a reporter at an aviation magazine and became a part-time flight instructor. I was happiest when I was both writing and teaching people to fly.

Dad was very proud when I earned my wings, so I wore my flight school uniform to the funeral along with the flight jacket Dad gave me when I earned my commercial pilot certificate. The jacket, which had been a plain brown when I got it, was now covered with experience patches. When I wasn't at work, I was a co-pilot on a B-25 owned by a non-profit group that traveled around the country giving rides to veterans.

Laura, her husband and four sons, were at the cemetery. The boys were tall, dark, and lanky like their father, and just as high maintenance as their mother. I had as little contact with Laura and her family as I could, because my relationship with my sister had not really improved since childhood. It doesn't matter if you're related, there are just some people you don't like.

Dad's second wife, Amy, was there with her adult son Peter. Amy was a miserable shrew of a woman. Dad was husband number three. Dad proposed on the second date. He said it was love at first sight, but I think Dad was just tired of being alone in a three-bedroom house. Amy was in her seventies. She used Dad like he was a walking ATM. She insisted Peter, who was in his fifties, move in with them 'temporarily' when he lost his job. Temporarily turned out to be six years and counting.

I visited Dad just once a year, partly because the house had too many bad memories, and partly because Amy didn't like me.

She resented my relationship with Dad, and once she accused me of stealing her pearls. I told her she was mistaken. Dad told her she was mistaken. Dad called me a week later to tell me Amy found the pearls on the floor behind the dresser. She never apologized for accusing me.

While Laura's family and Amy were next to the grave for the condolence line, I ducked away to talk to the funeral director about putting an image of a bicycle on the stone in honor of Dad who loved to ride his bicycle. The stone had a treble clef on it for Mom who loved to sing, and it didn't seem fair that there wasn't something for Dad. I had just finished the discussion when Butch Mathews approached. I was surprised to see him.

"Morgan? It's me, Butch Mathews! I'm so sorry for your loss," he said, holding out his hand.

I shook his hand. "Thank you for coming. How did you find out?"

"The newspaper," Butch replied. "Ever since Mom died and Dad had his stroke, he makes me read the obituaries to him every morning. He says it is a good day when he isn't in them."

"Your dad had a stroke?" I asked, slightly stunned.

"Yeah, about six months ago. He's in a wheelchair now most of the time, because his balance isn't too good. The left side of his body is messed up, and his memory is sort of screwy," Butch explained. "Sometimes he thinks my mother is still alive, and he goes looking for her, or he thinks that Suzy is my mother."

"That sounds awful," I stammered.

"It is what it is," Butch shrugged ruefully and he looked around. "They are around here someplace."

I guess the color went out of my face, because Butch's eyes suddenly went wide. "Morgan! Are you okay?"

"Yeah, I just didn't get a lot of sleep last night," I lied. "Is Suzy still working in environmental law?"

Butch let out a snort and rolled his eyes. "Environmental law, my butt! Mom made that up because she wanted Suzy to be a lawyer. Suzy tried for a job at the San Francisco Aquarium but when that didn't work out, she went back to work at the marine animal rehab clinic. After Mom died she moved home to help Dad. She worked with us at the hardware store while she went back to school to get an industrial design degree. She designs environmentally friendly office space for small companies."

"No kidding?" I was impressed.

"Yep! We joke that Suzy throws in extra hardware for the solar panels so the guys that build these things have to come to us," he laughed. "I wish you could meet my wife and kids. I've told them about how you and Suzy were the super jocks of the neighborhood when we were growing up. You were better athletes than the boys!"

Butch moved on to talk to Laura, and I found myself talking to one of Dad's truck buddies. Just behind him was a woman with long gray hair in a single large braid behind her neck. She was pushing an old man in a wheelchair. The man was wearing a dark suit and slippers and had the same chin and eyes as she did. *This has to be Suzy and Mr. Mathews!* my mind screamed. Suzy wore black square-framed glasses now. She was dressed in black slacks and a blazer and she looked more like a grandmother than the girl jock I remembered.

"Which one are you? Are you Laura or Morgan?" Mr. Mathews squinted at me through wire-rimmed bifocals.

"Morgan," I replied, pointing to the leather name tag on my flight jacket that read *Morgan E. Flynn, Instructor Pilot*. "Laura is the one with the boys," I said, gesturing to my sister and her brood a few feet away.

Mr. Mathews leaned forward in his chair. "Do you know who I am?"

I wasn't sure if he was asking me because he wanted to know whether I knew him, or if he didn't know himself, so I glanced at Suzy who mouthed the words "Dennis Mathews" and gave me a look like I needed to play along.

"Of course, you're Mr. Mathews," I said, feeling my body tense. Was he going to start screaming at me?

"And you know who this is, don't you?" he laughed, gesturing over his shoulder. "You remember my daughter? You girls played sports together? Football, wasn't it?"

"Along with soccer, field hockey and baseball, Dad," Suzy chortled, holding her right hand out to me. "Suzanne Mathews." She said it as if we had never met before.

"Captain Morgan Flynn." I replied. The guys I worked with always addressed me as Captain, and right at that moment I wanted some sort of barrier between me and Suzanne, as she was now calling herself — and I figured Captain would do it.

"Captain?" Suzy repeated, surprised. "You do look very… official."

"Yes, ma'am," I shook her hand firmly. "Good to see you again, ma'am."

"Did you fly in the war?" Mr. Mathews asked, gesturing to my jacket. "My father was a radio operator on a B-17 out of England."

Suzy rolled her eyes, because I was clearly about seventy years too young, not to mention the wrong gender to have flown combat in World War II.

"I'm an instructor pilot. If you will please excuse me, I have more guests to greet," Before either one of them could say anything else I stepped away.

After the funeral people came to the house for the wake. There had been changes. The swimming pool had been filled in and my fort converted into a potting shed. I took refuge in my fort. The ladder was still there. Out of nostalgia, I climbed on to the roof just like I used to as a kid. It still had a great view of the neighborhood.

I heard someone approaching and the door to the fort opened.

"Morgan? Are you up there?" It was Suzy.

"Yes, ma'am," I replied, a squadron of butterflies launching in my stomach.

I heard Suzy start up the ladder, and then her head popped up through the hatch. She was smiling. "Permission to come aboard?"

"Permission granted," I said.

As she climbed onto the roof I studied her. There were more lines around her eyes and mouth than before, and she had a small horizontal scar on her throat. Her skin was tanned and weathered. She had removed her jacket to reveal a green short-sleeved blouse. I couldn't help but notice how skinny her arms were compared to mine. As it was warm I had removed my flight jacket and rolled my sleeves up to the elbows.

Suzy swung her legs over the side. "Hello, Morgan," she smiled at me.

"Hello, ma'am," I nodded at her.

"Ma'am? Oh!" Suzy winced and made a face like she'd just bitten into a sour apple. "Don't call me that!"

I was amused by her reaction. "I take it you don't like being called ma'am?" I chuckled.

"Goodness, no!" Suzy cringed and shook her head.

"Noted." I laughed and shrugged as I said, "I earned my ma'am. I'm good with it. Ma'am is a term of respect."

Suzy gave me a reproachful look. "Ma'am bothers me and feels like a barrier between us."

"If not ma'am then how should I address you?"

"How about you address me the same way I address you?" she suggested, putting a bony hand on my wrist and leaning toward me.

I was tempted to remind her that I had known her for decades and she had changed her first name at least three times. Instead I asked, "Do you want me to call you little perv?'"

Suzy looked surprised then let out a bark of laughter as she remembered the reference. "I forgot all about that!"

"I didn't," I said, staring off into space as I continued dramatically, "Seeing the pink bra was a life changing event! It made girls clinically stupid! You went into slow motion! They heard the Carpenters *Close to You* playing in their heads! The sun stopped its movement in the sky!"

Suzy was laughing so hard she was crying. She gasped for breath as she cried, "Please tell me you became a writer!"

"Yes, I did," I nodded, smiling.

"Thank God!" Suzy rolled her eyes skyward. "It would be a shame to waste that dramatic narrative talent!" Then she paused, frowning as she asked "I forget, were you one of the little pervs who went to pieces at the mere glimpse of my bra strap?"

"Oh God, no," I shook my head, "I was too young. You could have handed me your bra, and I wouldn't have known what to do with it. To me, your brassiere was sacrosanct," I added solemnly. I leaned back. "So... now that we have settled that, how do you wish me to address you since 'little perv' is off the table?"

"How about if you call me Suzanne and I'll call you Morgan?" she grinned.

"As you wish," I nodded, looking around. "What did you do with your father?"

Suzy waved dismissively. "I parked him in the living room near one of Laura's boys, the youngest one, I think? Dad thinks he's Butch and will keep talking to him until he falls asleep or the real Butch shows up."

"I thought he was going to yell at me," I said sheepishly.

"I wondered why you ran off at the cemetery," Suzy laughed. "Just so you know, Dad's mind has pretty much Swiss cheesed. Sometimes he yells at me for not putting oil in the car — the one he sold when I was in high school — and sometimes he thinks I'm my mother and he tells me about the wedding plans he's been making for us. I'm learning a lot about my parent's courting days."

"So I guess you finally made up?"

"Finally," she said ruefully. "We didn't speak for years after he found out I was gay. He wanted me to get married, have kids, all the rituals. He got over it after my mother died." she snorted. "He tolerated me when I worked in the hardware store."

"Mixing paint," I recalled. "We got the paint for the nursery from there."

"I remember," Suzy nodded.

"So... Butch says he's married with kids. He looks like he grew up okay."

"Yes! He's been clean and sober, going on twenty years now," Suzy said, sounding all the world like a proud older sister. "He's running the hardware store like a champ. He and Jane have been together for like a gazillion years, and they have two kids."

"Boys or girls?"

"One of each. Both are seventeen. He has twins."

"Twins!" I cried. "Seriously?"

Suzy started laughing again. "Yep! No reproductive technology, purely God-given!" She gave me an evil look. "Dad and I think Butch stood too close to the fertilizer in the garden department."

"Damn! Wish we'd had the conversation sooner! I was standing pretty close to him out at the cemetery! I hope I didn't get a contact pregnancy?" I looked at her with mock horror.

Suzy shook her head dismissively. "I wouldn't worry about it. I have a degree in biology, and I can assure you there is no such thing as a contact pregnancy."

"Is parthenogenesis a thing yet?" I asked. "Gator told me about it in college."

"Gator?" Suzy's face creased thoughtfully. "I think that name rings a bell?"

"Big blonde girl, played sweep for the North State field hockey club and worked at the radio station."

"I remember her! What was the name of that other big girl? The one who played forward and wore a lot of orange?"

"Fireball," I supplied. "And yes, I still call her Fireball. She's a professional nature photographer now. Married to a woman, they live in Eugene, Oregon. I'm still in touch with Gator too. She lives in San Francisco and teaches at the University of California in the political science department."

"Do they still call you Wolf?"

"Oh yes! I was a bridesmaid at Gator's wedding. I was listed in the program as Wolf."

Suzy smiled warmly. "They were always very protective of you."

"Fireball always said, 'the pack takes care of its own'."

Suzy nodded sagely. There was a pause, and I could tell that Suzy was building up to something.

"You doing okay, Morgan?" she asked gently.

"Do you mean with Dad dying? Or in general?" I forced a lilt in my voice.

Suzy sighed and put her hand on my back in a comforting gesture. In spite of myself, I stiffened — and she felt it. She looked surprised as she quickly withdrew her hand. "I'm sorry! I didn't mean to make you uncomfortable."

"You didn't, you just surprised me," I said quickly. "I'm not a terribly physical person — well, except for sports. I still play field hockey."

Suzy raised her eyebrows. "Let me guess, you're still in the goal?"

"Of course."

"You never wanted to play anything but goalie," she chuckled.

"Not true," I corrected. "That semester the community college offered indoor field hockey as an intramural sport you and Linda sneaked me onto the team I played midfield."

"Were you any good?" Suzy frowned as if trying to recall it.

"Probably not," I shook my head. "But it did make Mom back off for a bit. During a Gourmet Group event at your parent's house Mom cornered you to ask why I was so stressed out. I think I was sleepwalking. You told her it was because I was trying to play at the college level when I was a first-year player."

"Did she buy it?" Suzy asked, looking amused.

"I think so," I shrugged. "She backed off a little after that?"

"Huh," Suzy shrugged and then gave me a look. "Why were you stressed out?"

The truth was I was stressed out because of the way Laura and Mom were constantly attacking me, but I didn't feel like reliving that, so I replied "Like I remember? It was probably something horrible and life-altering, like I saw my boyfriend talking to another girl," I said dramatically.

"Oh, I totally get that," Suzy nodded her head slowly. "That would have so been the end of the world for me too at that age."

"Or maybe I was stressed out after Coach Norton yelled at me when I was wearing nothing but a towel?" I suggested, remembering the day it happened to me — and Suzy. I looked at her. "That was a bad day."

"That would also do it for me," Suzy agreed, nodding empathetically now. "Hell, it did do it for me," she closed her eyes tight and shuddered. "Twice!"

"Twice?" I repeated, surprised.

"Oh yes," Suzy continued, still cringing. "It happened more than once, which is why I knew she meant business that time with you!"

I paused, getting a mental image of teenage Suzy walking the three blocks to home wearing nothing but one of those white gym towels that barely covered enough. I started to smirk and shake with suppressed laughter.

"You're picturing it, aren't you?" Suzy demanded, blushing and fighting a smile.

"Yes, ma'am! Sorry, ma'am!" I yelped, trying so hard to stop laughing. "Trying to think about something horrible! Famine! Rattlesnakes! Dead puppies!" I closed my eyes tight and wailed, "Mental image be gone!"

Suzy cleared her throat. I opened my eyes to find her looking at me with her arms folded on her chest. "Really? After all these years?" she demanded, looking annoyed.

"I have this vivid writer's imagination," I explained sheepishly. "Sorry?"

Suzy gave me a side look then addressed the sky as she howled, "IT.WAS.AWFUL!" She raised her hands on either side of her head as she continued "Thank GOD my brother and my father weren't home!"

"What did your mom say?"

"Nothing!" Suzy's eyes were wide. "I sneaked in the front door because I knew she'd be in the kitchen and ran up to my room and put on a pair of sweats before she even knew I was home!"

"How old were you?" I was amused. I had never heard this story before.

"Fourteen. A very stupid and immature fourteen!" Suzy had that look on her face, the same look she had the day of the swim party when Laura asked all those inappropriate questions about Butch.

"I'm just going to let my vivid writer's imagination go crazy," I said, biting back giggles. "I'm not going to ask what you did to get the White Towel Walk of Shame."

Suzy let out a whimper, then folded her arms on her chest and doubled over modestly. "Walk, my ass! I ran and ducked behind cars and bushes all the way home! It was November and cold and rainy too!"

"Damn!" I was impressed. "That explains so many things about the pink bra strap! I mean, what's the display of a bra strap when you've streaked the neighborhood?"

Suzy rolled her eyes and proclaimed solemnly, "Had I only known the power of my underwear, I would have used it for good and not for evil!"

We both laughed softly, then Suzy asked, "Do you remember the last time we were up here together?"

"Oh yes," I nodded. "He's thirteen. He's my brooooooooooooooother!" I wailed in my best imitation of fifteen-year-old Suzy.

"As I recall, you were ten and boys were still icky," She gave me a teasing look as she asked, "Did that change for you, or are they still icky?"

"They have their place," I replied with a shrug.

"Of course," Suzy replied, nodding. Then she sort of looked at me askance as she asked timidly, "Is there anyone? I don't see a ring on your left hand?"

There was an awkward silence and I closed my eyes, gathering my thoughts. I didn't like talking about relationships. I gave up on them a long time ago. I opened my eyes and staring straight ahead, I replied, "Flynn, Morgan E., Captain, 2732926."

Suzy let out sort of a squeak. "Did you just give me your name, rank, and serial number?"

"Yes, ma'am!" I barked. "It seemed like the best course of action. Perhaps we should go back to the pink bra?"

"It does seem to be the safest topic for discussion?" Suzy agreed, patting my hand. "I'm sorry, I didn't mean to touch a nerve."

"Did you marry?" I asked, trying to divert her attention.

Suzy chuckled ruefully. "You know that joke 'what does a lesbian bring on the second date? A U-Haul'? It's true!"

"Is it now?" I grinned. I'd heard this before.

"Oh yes," Suzy said confidently. "Thank God we couldn't legally marry when I was just coming out, because I would have been married like twenty times, and I swear that every time I was in love!"

She proceeded to tell me about her romantic life, beginning with how devastated she was when Winnifred decided she was no longer interesting, the men she had experimented with, and the women she rebounded with. There was the one that got away and broke her heart, and the one she called 'the bad break-up' that drained her bank account, physically assaulted her and shot her dog. Her stories made me glad I was single. For me, relationships seemed to be about the other person trying to change me or control me. The minute that happened, I would cut ties. I said as much to Suzy, and she responded by telling me about her wife, Mariah.

"After the bad break-up, I made a list of things I wanted in a relationship and what was negotiable. Then along came Mariah. We've been together for the past seven years," Suzy sighed. "I still have that list, and if my head gets turned, I go back to it to remind myself." She gave me a look. "I could dig it out and share it with you if you like?"

"Not necessary," I shook my head, uncomfortable at the suggestion.

She told me about Connie, the little girl she and Mariah had adopted as a baby. Connie was now five. As Mariah was thirty-two and as Suzy had just turned fifty, when they were out as a family she was often mistaken for Mariah's mother and Connie's grandmother. "I guess it's better than nothing," Suzy shrugged. "I would have liked to have some children of my own, but I am glad we have her,"

"That's nice," I replied, hearing a lot of pain in what she said.

We were quiet for a few minutes, then Suzy took a deep breath, bracing herself before she began somberly, "Morgan, I think we need to talk about that night on the overpass."

"We don't have to," I said quickly as a knot formed in my gut. I didn't want to think about that night much less talk about it.

"Morgan! Please!" Suzy's voice trembled. "Please, I need to talk about it! I've been carrying this for more than twenty years!"

I glanced at her. Her eyes were misty.

Reflexively, I reached behind her back and grabbed the tail of her blouse with my left hand.

"What are you doing?" she sputtered.

"Going with my strengths," I said, then added in my 'pilot' voice, "In the event of an unauthorized gravity check, I want to be prepared. I can use this crazy Amazon strength of mine to hang on to you if you try to go over the side?" I meant it as a joke, but it fell flat.

Suzy started to cry. "Morgan, no! Is this the best you've got? You're making jokes? I get it, you're uncomfortable, but stop with the jokes! Please stop with the jokes and little quips!"

Abashed, I released my grip and moved away from her, folding my hands in my lap. "I'm sorry. I didn't mean to make quips and it wasn't a joke. I really would try to keep you from going over the side." I shook my head. "I know you weren't yourself that night. You were chemically compromised."

Suzy let out a sniff and glanced at me. "You make it sound so clinical."

There was a lump in my throat suddenly, and I rushed on with, "But I always wondered what happened. You were gone the next morning before I woke up. And then you left my sweatshirt on my doorstep, no note, no phone call, no nothing!"

Suzy bowed her head as she said softly, "I didn't know what to say. I was embarrassed."

"You scared me!" I yelped, surprising both of us with the volume.

"I'm sorry," Suzy whimpered.

"For years I've wondered what put you out on the bridge that night. Did I do that? Was it my fault?" I wiped away tears with the back of my hands. "I've got to tell you, Suzy, that experience really sucked!"

Suzy's head snapped around and her voice was shrill with anger as she shouted, "I just wanted the pain to stop! Bootsy lived in the same apartment complex as me and I think we were walking home."

"With the BC girl you were going to bed," I muttered bitterly. "And as you went across the bridge you bolted for the hole in the fence."

"It was a mistake," Suzy's voice was strained and full of hurt as she continued, "I was in a bad place and I wanted it to be over. When I saw the hole in the fence it seemed like a way out."

I felt a tear slide down my face as I said, "Suicide is a permanent solution to temporary problems."

"What?" Suzy stared at me like I had just said something profound. "Where did you get that from?"

"That's what Britany told me suicide was," I explained. "You remember her — the team captain. I thought it was my fault you went out on the overpass," my voice was thin and I started to shiver. "Britany said I needed to talk to someone about it. She made me a couple of appointments at the campus counseling center."

Suzy's eyes went wide. "Really?"

"Yeah. She made appointments for Gator and Fireball and Bootsy too, along with a bunch of other people on the team."

"Oh my God!" Suzy cried, looking aghast.

"Bootsy was mad at me for not warning her about your ecstasy use. We didn't speak for weeks after that night. I even skipped hockey practice for like a month."

Suzy let out sort of a snort and gave me a sharp look. "You do tend to runway rather than deal with things."

Her words made me stiffen. "What's that supposed to mean?" I demanded. "You're the one that up and disappeared!"

"Oh, good God!" Suzy shrieked to the sky. "Quit saying that!

I didn't disappear! I dropped out of school! Don't make it sound so dramatic!"

"It was dramatic!" I argued. I shook my head. "I couldn't figure out why you wanted to die! You had a job waiting for you in San Francisco, they were paying for you to finish your masters — it seemed like it was a good thing! What happened? Did I hurt you that bad?"

Suzy glared at me as she said savagely, "It wasn't about you! I was lonely and isolated. I had no support system! My parents had disowned me, Fred had moved on and I moved from a vibrant city full of friends to an isolating shit-hole cow college like North State!"

"Shit-hole cow college?" I repeated, offended.

"I was anorexic too," Suzy continued. "It put me in the hospital. The doctor told my parents that about sixty percent of me wanted to die."

"Whoa, I knew you were damn skinny," I shuddered. "I'm glad you saw a doctor."

"So am I. After I got out of the hospital, I saw a therapist three times a week for a few months."

"Wow," I said, thinking that was an awful lot of couch time. "I guess it helped?"

"Yeah," Suzy sniffed, throwing me a look. "Did therapy help you?"

"I didn't go. I was embarrassed and ashamed at the suggestion so I didn't keep the appointments."

Suzy looked horrified. "Embarrassed and ashamed for getting therapy?" she cried. "Why?"

I squirmed. "It made me feel weak, and like I was being punished."

Suzy blinked. "Again, why?"

"I don't know," I shrugged. "Gator and Fireball said they felt the same way. Maybe it's a butch girl thing?"

Suzy let out a cry, then buried her face in her hands as she wailed, "I didn't know I hurt so many people!"

"You didn't mean to," I said quickly, moving over so I could put my arm around her. "You had a lot on your shoulders. The last hope of the Mathews family and all that."

Suzy made a choking noise and jerked away from me. "Oh fuck, not this again!" Her eyes narrowed in anger as she spat "I bet you think your family is some Hallmark movie of the week!"

I drew back, stung by the look of scorn she was giving me. "No..." I said slowly. "Quite frankly, this is probably the last time I will see the step-monster and Laura and her brood."

"Running away again, eh, Morgan?" Suzy sneered.

"It's my choice," I countered. "Laura and the step-monster I can do without altogether. Did you hear about the time the step-monster covered the house with gingerbread?"

"Gingerbread?" Suzy repeated, confused.

"Yes. Gingerbread," I said with a straight face. "Then she invited the neighborhood kids into the kitchen and tried to eat them."

Suzy's face darkened. She obviously didn't appreciate my humor. "Morgan, there is something wrong with you that you need to make jokes all the time! It's hiding a deep pain that you really should talk to someone about! And I mean this time, put in some effort. Actually talk to the therapist!"

I was half-annoyed, half-amused by her statement.

"No," I shook my head. "Don't want it, don't need it."

Suzy disagreed. "You make jokes to hide your anger and your pain. You're afraid to let people see your heart!"

"I have no idea what you're talking about," I said. "Why is this so important to you?"

"Because you're pretending to be okay when you're not!" Suzy shrieked. "Just like when you were a kid! You need to find someone to talk to about this, because I can't help you!"

I stared at her. "When did this become about you?" I asked, my voice dripping with resentment. "You do realize, of course, that I buried my father today? My last parent? And I might be just a little upset? Is that okay with you? Do I have your permission to be upset?"

Suzy glared at me. "Are you fucking with me?" she demanded.

I sighed. "No. I would not fuck with you without written permission, obtained three weeks in advance," I replied tersely, then I grabbed my jacket and I jumped off the fort to the walkway below. It was only a seven-foot drop – I had done the jump many times as a kid. "We're done here. Stay up there as long as you want, I'm leaving."

"Of course you are!" Suzy cried, then she was scrambling down the ladder. She burst out of the fort yelling at me. "You know what, Morgan? You haven't changed at all! You're still insecure and dramatic like you were as a kid! You run away from things rather than dealing with them!"

Her words brought me up short. I turned to face her. "A couple of things: first off, I am no longer a kid. Second, when I was fourteen I was insecure and dramatic. That is age appropriate for girls," I said, biting off each word. "That was then, this is now. I like who I am now, and I don't want or need your approval!"

"You're running away," Suzy said scornfully. "Rather than dealing with the issues, you're running away."

"I buried my father today and the last thing I need is the judgment of someone whose personality has to be chemically activated," I shot back. "I withdraw my previous statement. The idea of you performing a gravity check off the roof has some appeal. Be my guest! It's not an overpass over a freeway, but it will have to do."

Suzy gasped, and her lower lip was quivering as she said, "I'm going to pretend you didn't say that! I have a gun and a dog to protect me from people like you!"

"Then you better be a good shot," I growled, wondering how the conversation had taken such a dark turn.

Suzy shook her head. "I feel sorry for you if you have to rely on aggression! You are carrying around a lot of anger, and it's not healthy!"

"It's transitional," I replied. "I anticipate that when I get away from you the anger will dissipate."

Suzy put her hand on my arm. "Morgan, please! You might be so much happier if you got therapy to deal with all this anger?"

I jerked away from her. "Back off, Mathews!" I snarled. "What is making me angry right now is you. I am dealing with it by walking away from you. I am happy, well, not at this very moment, I mean because Dad died and all, and the fact you're being a judgmental bitch, but for the most part, I am happy and I like who I am!"

Suzy gave me a pained look. "I don't think so. You have always had difficulty relating to people. You tried to hide it as a kid, but you were scary smart and really, really sensitive. I remember all the crap Laura and your mother used to dump on you. You need to forgive them and let it go. A therapist could help you do that. I can see that you're in pain, still carrying it around like a duffle bag."

You know that expression 'triggered'? At that moment, I was the poster girl for it. Suzy wasn't hearing me. Just like Mom never heard me. Mom often accused me of cutting school or other self-destructive behaviors that I did not do. When I asked Mom where she got her (usually wrong) information about my activities she always replied, 'they told me'. I knew there was no 'they'. The few times I tried to talk to Mom — I mean really talk to her — about something that was bothering me she told me I did not feel that way, or that I was overreacting or intentionally trying to upset her. As a result, I learned not to talk to her — or anyone else — about anything of substance. I learned it was better to cut people like that out of my life.

"I did let it go! I left it behind me when I left home. Problem solved!" I argued.

"Problem came with you!" Suzy countered. "I'm willing to bet you've carried that baggage into every relationship you've ever attempted! I bet that's why you're still single!"

"I'm single by choice, not like it's any of your business," I snapped.

"You're Peter Pan!" Suzy cried. "It's time to grow up!"

"What the fuck are you talking about?" I demanded, utterly confused.

Suzy started to argue that she was saying this as my friend, but I cut her off with "No, you're not!" I took a step toward her, bellowing, "We are not friends! We have not been friends for decades! I am sick of your holier-than-thou attitude! How dare you come into this house on the day of my father's funeral and judge and attack me and my family!"

"This isn't an attack or a judgment!" Suzy stammered. "I know I'm in dangerous territory, but I really think that you'd get much more out of life if you got therapy to deal with all this anger. Therapy helped me quite a bit."

"I don't think it did," I said, and then I took the gloves off. "As I recall, you can't function unless you are chemically enhanced. Did you get past that? Or does your therapist write you a prescription?"

Suzy's eyes went wide, and she started to tremble. She started to walk away but I grabbed her arm and stopped her. I leaned in and continued in a harsh whisper in her ear, "You were a bully in high school, a bully in college and it doesn't appear that anything has changed. You still ignore boundaries. I've always wondered, when we were kids, were you grooming me? Did you want me in your bed even then? Think about it — what does a seventeen-year-old want with a twelve-year-old? Why did you insist on recruiting me for the field hockey team? What were you really after? It's always about control for you, isn't it, Mathews? Is that what this little discussion is? Is this about control, for you?" I let go of her arm and stepped back.

"You little fuck!" Suzy growled.

"It's bothered me for years," I continued. "Or maybe it was Mom you liked? I have to know — did you and Mom have a Mrs.

Robinson affair going on? I always thought Mom was so far back in the closet she was a garment bag — did you scratch that itch?"

All the color drained from Suzy's face and she appeared to be having an asthma attack or at least gasping for air as she croaked out, "I can't believe you just said that! How completely unthinkable and completely inappropriate!"

I cocked my head to one side. "I'm not hearing a denial. Get off the high horse, Mathews! If she was good enough for Dad, she was good enough for you!"

That did it. Suzy slapped me across the face so hard it made me stumble, then before I knew what I was doing, I grabbed her right wrist and twisted her arm behind her back forcing her to her knees. I stood behind her, squeezing her right wrist with all my strength as I knelt on her back, pushing her face down onto the concrete walkway.

"That was a stupid thing to do, Mathews!" I shouted.

Suzy protested and cried out in pain. "You're hurting me!"

"That's the idea," I said, tightening my grip and putting my left hand on the back of her neck. My voice was eerily calm as I said, "We're not kids anymore. You try to hurt me I don't have a problem hurting you. In fact, I think it might do you a world of good to be physically damaged so you understand pain, and what your words do to people."

Suzy struggled. "I swear to God, Morgan! Let go!" she screamed.

"You need to learn boundaries, Mathews. When you hurt someone, especially physically hurt someone, don't be surprised if and when they hurt you back," I slipped my left hand around her throat. Her flesh was warm against my fingers, and I squeezed her throat slowly. I felt her pulse quicken as I continued, "When I let go of you, you are going to get your father and Butch and you will leave this house and never come back. If you ever fuck with me or even one of my friends again, I will tie you to the railroad tracks and let the train cut you in half." It was the ugliest thing I could think of, and from the noise Suzy made, I think she appreciated that.

"Fuck you!" she croaked when I released her.

"Not really looking for a relationship right now," I said, stepping back quickly. I brought my hands up in a defensive posture, just in case she tried to swing on me again.

But Suzy was in no condition to fight back. Her face was purple and crumpled in tears. She reached for her throat with her left hand and painfully and slowly pulled her right arm to her body. There were red marks on both her throat and wrist. She gagged and coughed a few times and then looked up at me, so hurt and bewildered as she warbled, "Do you feel better now, Morgan?"

"Yeah, I do," I lied. "That's what it feels like to be hurt, Suzy. Since you didn't seem to be listening, I felt a practical application was called for."

"Violence is never called for!" Suzy cried, staggering to her feet.

"It was self-defense," I grinned with false bravado. Inside I was sick. I had just destroyed my childhood hero. "Go away, Mathews," I said curtly as I turned to walk away. "I never want to see you again."

"Go in peace, Morgan," Suzy sobbed.

CHAPTER 21

Come Fly With Me

It was early Sunday morning when someone identified as BTM sent me a message on Facebook. "Good morning, I hope this does not wake you. Is this Morgan Flynn who attended Wilson High School?"

"Yes, I am that person." I replied.

"Hooray! This is Butch Mathews – do you remember me? Suzy's little brother?"

I stared at the computer screen. Of course I remembered him. The last time I saw him was at Dad's funeral several years earlier.

"I remember you," I replied, a chill rolling over me. It was bad enough that I buried my father that day. The fight I had with his sister still haunted me. I found it spooky that she would come back on my radar at this particular time, as a week earlier I had started to play field hockey again. It had been years since I picked up a stick. Ironically, it was a life-changing injury that brought me back to the game. Three years ago I injured my back — I still don't know exactly how — I felt sore one night and the next day woke up in excruciating pain and unable to stand. I called work to tell them I couldn't come in because I had lost the use of my legs. Within an hour I was in the emergency room — one of my coworkers took me. In the weeks that followed my coworkers and former students — my airport family — took turns taking me to doctor appointments, physical therapy, bringing me groceries, etc. I had no idea that I had that kind of support system in place, but it was appreciated. I felt loved and vowed to be a better person.

The injury came on the heels of a relationship break up — her name was Cassidy, and she was also a pilot. We'd been together for the better part of three years, but had grown apart when she went off to the airlines. We tried an LDR, but it became clear the relationship had run its course, so we split. We never moved in together (although we did talk about it a lot) and I said I was okay letting her go, but I guess I wasn't, because according my doctor, I got injured because I didn't properly grieve and I didn't listen to my body or my heart. Recovery was a long road, and I was still on it. I did daily physical therapy. The only good thing about the injury was that it helped me shift my perspective. I made more time for friends and things that brought me joy — field hockey was one of those things. It took three years, five days, and two surgeries to return to the pitch. I figured that was pretty good for a woman who was looking at her fiftieth birthday in the rearview mirror. I was always afraid it would be taken away from me again so in addition to the PT twice a day I walked three miles a night and made more time for a social life. I was never going to take my friends or physical well-being for granted again.

I hesitated before I continued the conversation. "How are the wife and kids?"

He answered right back. "The family is well. My wife is still as beautiful as ever, and the twins are about to turn 24! Are you still in the Seattle area and still flying?"

"Yes."

We continued to message back and forth for the next half-hour. Butch did most of the talking. He told me Butch Junior was an apprentice plumber and training to take over the family business. His daughter Ricki-Lyn was about to graduate from college and was trying to get into the Air Force as a pilot.

"Suzy thought you might be a good resource for her." Butch wrote. "Suzy said you were a pilot in the Air Force?"

I replied I was not, although I helped train some of their pilots. My stomach tightened as I typed. It still made me uncomfortable to think about Suzy. I still felt bad about the fight we'd had. Part of me wanted to apologize, and over the years there were a few times I started writing a letter to her, but I talked myself out of it every time. I wanted to forget about that day, and I figured she did too.

Butch asked about my life. I told him I had been able to take two passions, writing and flying, and make careers out of them. These days I mostly taught flying. I told him about the injury and learning to walk again, and how excited I was when I started playing hockey again. I told him that playing as an adult was so much more emotionally fulfilling than it had been playing as a kid, and how I got to practice an hour before the rest of the team to do strengthening and agility drills.

"Suzy would be so proud!" he replied.

I felt sad when I read that. She was the first person I thought of when I joined the team. I reached out to Gator, Fireball and Linda to tell them I was playing again. They were happy for me. I wondered how Suzy would react if I contacted her. The bridge had not been burned, it was nuked from orbit by both of us. She pushed and I pushed back. In my mind's eye, I could still see Suzy on her knees with her right arm twisted behind her back and my left hand tightening around her throat. It frightened me that I had, on some level, enjoyed hurting her, and I was ashamed of that. It made me aware of how dangerous my temper was. Since then, I had learned to remove myself from situations before I reached that level of rage. The rage did, however, have an upside. When physically threatened I had a tendency to act, not react. I learned this when a strung out druggie tried to rob the flight school one night. It was just me and another woman working. The would-be robber threatened my coworker with the monkey wrench. As he drew back to hit her I grabbed a fire extinguisher off the wall and slammed him in the face so hard it broke his nose and knocked him out. After that my boss referred to me as 'the female Chuck Norris'. It was not a title I was proud of.

The online conversations continued for several weeks with Butch mostly asking for advice to help his daughter become a pilot. I suggested books she should read. I was very careful not to bring up Suzy in conversation, or even react when he mentioned her. Butch noticed and commented on it one day saying, "I told Suzy I was in touch with you now. She finally told me what REALLY happened at your father's funeral. She told me that when she goes to commercial airports and sees a woman in a pilot's uniform she always hopes it is you.".

I didn't know what to say to that.

"She's really sorry about the fight you two had. She said her timing was terrible and she felt awful because you were so sad that day," he continued. "She's sorry that she antagonized you. She says she was out of line."

"I'm not sorry that I defended myself," I replied.

"She says you saved her life when you were both at North State. She would have died that night if you hadn't been there."

Tears stung my eyes. "That was a long time ago," I wrote. "With all due respect, Butch, with friends like Suzy, I don't need enemies."

"She's not who she was," Butch replied, then proceeded to tell me about Suzy getting what he described as "her karmic payback", starting with a car accident attributed to driving while impaired. She was in her 50s and still partying like a 20-year-old. She had Connie in the car at the time. Neither of them was seriously hurt, but Mariah was furious. A short time later Mr. Mathews died in his sleep and Suzy was diagnosed with breast cancer. It was Suzy's second bout of cancer and Mariah said she couldn't go through it again and left, taking Connie with her.

"I think Mariah left because of the accident cand used the cancer as an excuse," Butch said, adding that Suzy came to the realization that universe was trying to teach her something. "She turned her life around," he continued. "She had some addiction issues so she went to therapy to work on repairing herself. She went around making amends as she prepared for surgery and possibly her death. She drew up a will, set up a trust fund for Connie, made her own funeral arrangements, then underwent a radical mastectomy. She had made peace with the world and was prepared to leave it," said Butch, "But God had other plans."

The surgery was a success, he said, and the recovery was brutal, but it worked — Suzy had been cancer free for two years. During her convalescence she took classes online and now had a degree in counseling. "She works with gay teens who have addiction issues. She knows where they are coming from," Butch explained. "She's also in a healthier relationship with someone closer to her own age, and has shared custody of Connie now. I'm really proud of her for the way she's turned her life around."

So am I, I thought.

"Do you think you could make peace? You're both in your fifties now and you would think you could let bygones be bygones?" There was a line of sad emojis. "She asks about you. It sounds like you've both had your trials and matured. Don't you think if you talked you could iron things out? You're not kids anymore."

I had a lump in my throat as I crafted my reply. "I don't know. We weren't kids at the funeral, yet Suzy didn't seem to accept me as an adult," I reminded him. "She ignored boundaries and I don't have the patience for that. I think it's best to leave her in the past. However, I will admit when there is a conversational reference to a pink bra, I do immediately think of her."

One day Butch messaged that he was coming up to Seattle

for business. He planned to bring Ricki-Lyn with him. Would I be around on such-and-such date and such-and-such a time, and could I take his daughter for a flight?

I knew having some flight time logged would increase her chances of getting a pilot's slot in the Air Force, so I said yes and gave him the address of the flight school. A week later I was at my desk at the flight school when Boss, the big, gray-haired ex Navy guy that owned the school called me to say my 11 o'clock had arrived. I just about fainted when I walked into the lobby. It was them. Butch had slimmed down and lost quite a bit of hair, but that wasn't the shocking part. Ricki-Lyn looked exactly like Suzy had in her early twenties. I was so startled I dropped into a defensive posture.

"I see you notice the resemblance?" Butch chuckled as I pulled myself together.

"Yes! Wow!" I exclaimed, looking at the dark-haired young woman standing before me dressed in jeans and a green t-shirt.

Butch proudly put his arm around his daughter. "Except for the blue eyes — she gets those from her mother — she looks just like my sister Suzy did at that age."

"Is that a good thing?" Ricki-Lyn asked, glancing at her father then at me.

"Yes, yes it is," I said, holding out my hand. "My name is Morgan. I'll be your instructor on this flight. I grew up with your father and his sister. I've known your father since he thought girls were icky."

That made them laugh.

I took Ricki-Lyn out to the Cessna 172, and Butch waited inside the office. I showed Ricki-Lyn how to use the checklist to do a preflight inspection of the aircraft. Once the airplane was deemed airworthy, I asked her if she wanted her father to come along. She said yes, so I strapped Butch into the backseat.

Intro flights have a protocol. I do the takeoff and landing, because the one thing I can't fix is if the client inadvertently activated the brakes by pressing on the tops of the rudder pedals. The airplanes have dual controls so I can fly, or the client can fly. Once we were up at a thousand feet, I put my hands in the air and said, "Your airplane, your controls!" and the client takes over. I am always ready to jump back on — and I have had to a few times when the client tried to pull a fighter-pilot move like they do in a video game. Real training airplanes don't work like that, and that makes it a dangerous thing to do, especially close to the ground.

Ricki-Lyn took direction well. I gave her headings and altitudes to fly, and she repeated them back to me as she flew them, telling me she'd been studying the books I suggested. I was impressed. Butch was holding his cellphone up and capturing the whole flight on video.

Ricki-Lyn was doing such a good job I invited her to try the landing, telling her I would coach her. I said I still had lightning-fast field hockey goalie reflexes and I would grab the controls if I needed to.

"She means that, Ricki-Lyn!" Butch chortled from the back seat. "Your Aunt Suzy recruited her for the Wilson team."

"I played field hockey in high school!" Ricki-Lyn grinned at me. "I played midfield and sometimes forward."

Just like Suzy, I thought.

The landing was darn near perfect. We touched down on the

centerline and I tapped the brakes. With some coaching from me, Ricki-Lyn made the last radio call announcing that we were clear of the runway.

As we were taxiing up to the school ramp, Butch pointed to a woman dressed in khakis and an orange windbreaker standing on the other side of the fence. She was wearing sunglasses and had gray hair cut in a short bob. "Speaking of Suzy…" he said sheepishly.

"I had a feeling," I muttered, butterflies manifesting in my stomach.

Butch leaned forward and touched my shoulder. "Keep an open mind," he said softly.

I gave him a look.

We shut down the airplane, and as Ricki-Lyn handed me the keys I asked, "Did you have a good time?"

"It was awesome!" Ricki-Lyn screamed. She was grinning from ear to ear.

Boss opened the gate and escorted Suzy on to the ramp. He led her around to Ricki-Lyn's side of the aircraft. Ricki-Lyn jumped out of the cockpit and into Suzy's arms, crowing about how much fun she'd had and how cool it was to be a pilot. Suzy looked highly amused at her niece's exuberance.

I glanced back at Butch.

"I think she's going to be a pilot," I grinned.

"I hope so," Butch's voice cracked with emotion.

"Are you okay?" I asked.

"Sure," Butch said, grinning as he wiped away tears. "It's just not every day you see your little girl realize her dream."

"Of course. Take all the time you need," I said, stepping out of the airplane. This was the best part of the job for me — seeing people realize their dreams.

Boss pushed Ricki-Lyn next to me for the obligatory client and pilot photo next to the airplane pose, then he gestured to Suzy who was standing off to the side. "Morgan! I believe you two know each other?"

"Yes, we do," I said, nervously.

Suzy was blushing as she removed her sunglasses. Her eyes were misty. "Hello Spunky," her voice was husky.

"Spunky?" Boss repeated, amused.

"High school nickname," I said, feeling my pulse quicken. "Hello, Traffic Ticket."

"I'm wearing a pink bra," Suzy announced dramatically, drawing a look of confusion from Boss and Ricki-Lyn.

"I would expect nothing less," I replied solemnly.

Suzy's lower lip trembled. "I'm sorry!" she cried, cutting right to the chase.

"I know," I replied, my voice breaking. "So am I."

"May I hug you?" Suzy asked tearfully, holding her arms open.

"I'd be awfully disappointed if you didn't," I admitted, and we fell into each other's arms.

"Aw, Spunky," Suzy sobbed. "I'm so sorry!"

"I know," I cried. "I'm sorry too! I've missed you, Traffic Ticket!"

"Fuck us both for being stupid!" Suzy bawled savagely.

I leaned back so I could look her in the eye. "Oh, quit crying! You're going to get us kicked out of the Junior Amazon League!"

"We're Wildcat tomboys, we can cry if we want to!" Suzy answered defiantly, then let out the Wildcat growl.

I responded with a growl of my own, then leaned back and let out a howl like a wolf calling to the pack.

Suzy, still with her arms around me, replied with a louder, longer growl and I answered. We understood each other perfectly.

Boss and Ricki-Lyn and the few other people who were witnessing the reunion looked perplexed.

Butch, now out of the airplane, stood there, smiling smugly. "Yeah...that's what I figured would happen," he told his daughter.

"Dad...what language are they speaking?" Ricki-Lyn asked.

"If I'm not mistaken... I think that is Wildcat?" Butch suggested with a tearful smile. Then he addressed the small crowd, announcing dramatically "This is normal for them! This is what they do!"

"Is it a tribal greeting?" Boss asked suspiciously.

Suzy and I shared a look as I said, "You could call it that."

"What tribe is that?" Boss prompted.

While looking at each other, Suzy and I replied in unison,

"The Tomboys of Cherry Lane!"